DEEP BLUE ALM°ST BLACK

THANASSIS VALTINOS

TRANSLATED FROM THE GREEK BY JANE ASSIMAKOPOULOS
AND STAVROS DELIGIORGIS

HYDRA BOOKS NORTHWESTERN UNIVERSITY PRES

DEEP BLUE ALMOST BLACK

SELECTED FICTION

VANSTON, ILLINOIS

Hydra Books
Northwestern University Press
Evanston, Illinois 60208-4210

First paperback printing 2000

Printed in the United States of America

ISBN 0-8101-1766-5

Earlier versions of "Nekuia: Journey to the Dead" and "There Still Is a God" appeared in *World Letter* 6 (1995): 17–18; "August '48" in *London Magazine* 36, nos. 1 and 2 (April–May 1996): 11–16; "August '48," "The River Káystros," "Peppers in a Flowerpot," "Panayotis," and "Autumn Storm" in *Iowa Review* 26, no. 2 (May 1996): 11–37; "The Stepfather" in *Athenian* (July 1996): 40–42; translations by Jane Assimakopoulos and Stavros Deligiorgis.

Library of Congress Cataloging-in-Publication Data
Valtinos, Thanasēs
       [Tha vreite ta osta mou hypo vrochēn. English]
       Deep blue almost black : selected fiction / [Thanassis Valtinos].
       p. cm.
  ISBN 0-8101-1766-5 (pbk. : alk. paper)
  I. Assimakopoulos, Jane. II. Deligiorgis, Stavros, 1933– . III. Title.
  PA5633.A4P4813 1997
  889'.334—dc21   97-2208
                                                         CIP

CONTENTS

Thanassis Valtinos was born in an Arcadian village in the Peloponnesus in 1932. He studied political science, briefly, and film, served as an officer in the reserves, and held various jobs in the harbor of Piraeus and in Athens. He first achieved national recognition with the publication of some of his work in the late 1950s and early 1960s, most notably his widely read novella *The Descent of the Nine*.

International recognition soon followed in 1970 with the award of a Ford Foundation grant for creative writing, accompanied by invitations abroad to the Deutscher Akademischer Austauschdienst (Berlin, 1974–75, 1987) and the International Writing Program at the University of Iowa (Iowa City, 1976), where he is an honorary fellow. He is also a member of the European Academy of the Sciences and the Arts (Salzburg) and the International Theater Institute.

His work, which includes long and short fiction of all types, has been translated into many European languages. He travels extensively and has received numerous awards for his work, both in Greece and abroad, the latest for his book *Data on the Decade of the Sixties*, which won the Greek State Literature Prize in 1989 and was short-listed for the European Literature Prize in 1991.

In Greece, his work as a novelist earned him the position of president of the Society of Greek Writers, a post he held for many years. He is also a member of the Greek Society of Playwrights, and his translations of classical Greek drama—many of which were written for the Art Theater of the late Karolos Koun—are performed at annual festivals at Epidaurus and other ancient theaters throughout Greece. His novels, plays, and film scripts, including the award-winning script of the film *Voyage to Kythira* (Cannes Film Festival, 1984), written in collaboration with the distinguished Greek film director Theodoros Angelopoulos, have established him as one of the most versatile and talented men of letters in Greece today.

The twelve short stories in *You Will Find My Bones Under Rain* were written between 1960 and 1991. Some were originally published in various literary journals, while others appeared for the first time in the collection *Tha vreite ta osta mou ypo vrohin (You Will Find My Bones Under Rain*, Athens, 1992). The stories are printed here in the strict chronological order in which they were written. As such, they can be viewed as an artist's documentation of a period of fierce and often brutal change for modern Greece as a whole. In the background of these stories lie the major dislocations of three generations of Greeks: from the time of the Asia Minor catastrophe in 1923, when some one and a half million Greeks from western Turkey flooded the Greek mainland and its islands, through the German occupation of Greece during the Second World War, the ensuing civil war (1947–49), and the seven-year-long military dictatorship (1967–74), all of this accompanied by large-scale migration of Greeks to northern Europe, America, and Australia.

The Greek artists who lived through this ongoing nightmare—the better ones at least, including not only prose writers like Valtinos but also the Nobel Prize–winning poets George Seferis and Odysseus Elytis—have consistently practiced the decencies of the survivor: No grandiose words for a people who have repeatedly shown themselves to be so vulnerable from the outside as well as from the inside. There could be no illusions before the unceasing disemboweling of Greece, the tearing down of every dream and every humane expectation. Indeed, Valtinos's stories contain neither grandiose words nor illusions. They are, simply put, prosaic stories about Greece and about the Greeks—a country and a people possessed of both antiquity and contemporaneity.

The opening two stories, "August '48" and "The River Káystros," seem to make up a contrastive pair, literally an antiphon: the first being cast mainly in the "Doric" style, with its measured volumes of strife and transcendence; the second, more lyrical, more "Ionic" in tone, concerns love and family in the final months of the Nazi occupation of Athens, but ends in the more pedestrian present of bargains and flea markets. Valtinos is not above exposing the Greece of the second half of the twentieth century with its nightclubs and pulp magazines ("Roses for Maria A."), nor will he spare consumerist Greece its torturers, coups, and political deportees of the same period ("Peppers in a Flowerpot," "The Plaster Cast"). The Greece of visions in "Nekuia: Journey to the Dead," where a truck driver has a prophetic dream about his own near death, and the ghostly apparitions and saints' shrines in the middle of olive groves in "You Will Find My Bones Under Rain," come as a surprise, at least to the reader who has no insight into the popular religion of this sun-drenched landscape.

The latter story, from which this collection takes its name, is an excellent example of Valtinos's art as well as his choice of content. The account has all the marks of a slightly illiterate gendarme's report to his superiors but turns imperceptibly into a chronicle as it lists dates and "facts," such as field laborers hearing groans from a bag of newly disinterred bones, people receiving visitations and prophetic utterances from forgotten martyrs, and, finally, the names of the chorus of women—and, of course, their husbands' names as well—who appear to be almost synchronized in their urge to establish the cult of a new saint. The establishment of a local hero's cult in Greek antiquity must have been a fairly similar process.

The story entitled "A Plaster Cast" reveals yet another facet of Valtinos's literary versatility. It first came out in a volume of work by eighteen writers and intellectuals (originally entitled *Eighteen Texts,* 1970) in defiance of the military dictatorship in power at that time. It can be seen, more specifically, as an allegory pure and simple, whose central metaphor is based on the very words the dictators often used to justify their abuses and oppression of the Greek people, who were repeatedly characterized as ailing "patients" in need of their expert "care."

An introductory note could not possibly do justice to Valtinos's range of themes, personae, and moods in the present collection. Suffice it to say that the layering of ironies charges almost every turn in the action of his stories. Civility makes an unexpected appearance in the interrogation chamber ("Peppers in a Flowerpot"), as pleasantries are exchanged between the commandant who is cultivating peppers in a flowerpot and the prisoner about to be interrogated, who silently compares the peppers to the gorse with which tyrants were flayed in ancient times, an allusion to Plato and also to Seferis. The erotic may suddenly peek through in the torture chamber ("The Plaster Cast") or in the derelict old age of a war veteran selling fertility herbs to the ladies in a provincial brothel ("Panayotis").

We are impressed by the ease with which Valtinos can draw us into a high-school teacher's neurotic introspection about a former lover ("Autumn Storm"), or the matter-of-fact description of the methodical process by which two former lovers enter the two-dimensional world of a photograph in order to gain access to a time that can no longer be relived or experienced again ("There Still Is a God"). It is an art that will often assume the tones of an objective statement, say, to the police ("Roses for Maria A."), but which is, at the same time, capable of provoking the greatest depth of association and immediacy of feeling, as in the story "Peter and Pat," with its poignant finale. This story is an excellent illustration of the economy of means by which Valtinos creates complex but utterly believable worlds for his readers through the careful delineation of a wide range of characters, be they dreamers, fighters, lovers, or other miscast idealists.

In contrast to the short stories in *You Will Find My Bones Under Rain*, varied in content yet quite traditional in form, Valtinos's *Deep Blue Almost Black* is a "novella" in name only, by virtue of its size and etymological proximity to the term, as it was a refreshingly "new" work when it first appeared on the Greek literary scene under the title *Ble vathy shedon mavro* (Athens, 1985). Shorn as it is of the traditional elements of plot and story line, and lacking an author's mediating point of view, the work could more easily be described as a kind of "anti-novella." Its first-person, stream-of-consciousness narrative brings to mind a theatrical monologue, and *Deep Blue Almost Black* has, in fact, been performed as a kind of "one-act play," both in Greece and abroad.

As the novella opens, we are thrown headlong into the life of an anonymous yet strangely familiar Athenian woman as we "listen," like inadvertent eavesdroppers, to a long string of verbal (or is it written?) trivia about the narrator's difficulties sleeping at night, her chocolate-eating dog, and her incurably narcissistic first husband. The writer's craft comes into play precisely at the point where it achieves its greatest transparency. In just one short page we already think and speak of the aging heroine as if she were independent of the art that created her.

On and on she talks, we do not yet know to whom, about her childhood, which she still clings to tenaciously; her three failed marriages; her cold, hard mother whose portrait was ruined by a restorer; her hard-bargaining, "merchant" grandmother, who succeeds in purchasing a deathbed indulgence from the Patriarch of Alexandria to the tune of 10,000 gold sovereigns along with the right to be buried holding a braided silver purse containing the shriveled-up umbilical cords of her fourteen children.

As the monologue progresses, we are increasingly surprised by the nestled and layered worlds it uncovers, and by the sonorities and complex dissonances of the narrative voice itself—a unique blend of experience, fantasy, and wry self-deprecation. Brightly colored, well-crafted toys of Christmases past, exuberant, overweight cooks, and English headmistresses receive the same kind of attention as her first sexual encounter with a young Italian—a disappointing experience which she nonchalantly compares to dental work. In a carefully orchestrated transition, the trivial gradually gives way to the profound, as the narrator's deep-seated existential "ennui" begins to filter up through her protective facade of innocuous chatter. Slowly, we piece together the fragments of her insignificant life into a mosaiclike portrait of a deeply unhappy woman fallen prey to the strong emotions of midlife: uncertainty about everything she is or might have been; loneliness "seeping through her body like a low fever"; panic, which attacks and "overwhelms" her when she least expects it; anger at the passage of time and at her own memory, which never allows her to forget.

In the end, her memory "cannot be put aside," and in spite of all her talking and soul-searching, the deliverance of true communication evades her. The novella ends where it began, with the narrator imprisoned in a self she can neither escape from nor be comfortable with. The monologue is rife with images of entrapment—in beds, chairs, marriages, in language itself, and, especially, of the self by the self—an image that finds its ultimate expression in a "nightmarish painting" done by the narrator's "bohemian" friend Aigle, whose death she still mourns. It pictures two embryonic figures trapped in a Dantesque embrace. The colors of the painting, "deep blue, almost black," reflect her mood in the face of her own impending old age and death. At the close of the narrative she readies herself, once more, for darkness and a drug-induced sleep.

Much to his credit, Valtinos has created an unself-pitying narrator who, like the heroines in Seneca's heartbreaking tragedies for a single actress, repopulates her stage with spoiled children in the formal parks of France, sexually preoccupied adolescents in the mercantile communities of the Sudan, and restless adults of the Greek diaspora in modern Egypt, making utterly convincing music out of the accidents of time, fast-aging flesh, and the worlds within her worlds.

J. A.

S. D.

September 1996

YOU WILL FIND MY BONES UNDER RAIN

SHORT STORIES

Despite our failures we should not be troubled: It is not things that matter but our judgment about things. Besides, we are both dealers in nostalgia.

The captain asked for volunteers and three men stepped forward. The sergeant was a Macedonian and the other two were Peloponnesians. The captain took his binoculars and told them to approach him. They walked up to the abutment and crouched behind some rocks. Rising before them and facing them was the town of Voursiani. The captain began the briefing.

"Check the hill right in front of you. There is a goat trail to the left. On the side of it you can see a small landing. The shell crater is in the middle of the landing. The soil is reddish. The soldiers are lying face down around the crater, like men drinking water. Do you see them, sergeant?"

"Yes, captain, sir."

"How about the two of you?"

"Captain, sir."

"Here, take the binoculars."

The soldier held the binoculars a little awkwardly.

"Don't do anything to them. Hold them up to your eyes just as they are."

The sergeant turned and looked at the man holding the binoculars.

"OK, follow the goat trail," said the captain.

The soldier was a bit slow.

"Yes sir," he said, but his voice was somewhat uncertain.

"See the hill? The landing is right above it."

"Yes sir," the soldier said again.

The captain took a deep breath.

"See the crater in the middle?"

"Yes sir."

"The men have fallen down all around it. They look like they're drinking water."

The sergeant thought to himself: more like they were looking down into hell.

The soldier said nothing. His eyes had gotten used to the lenses. He stared motionless at the three almost shapeless bodies.

"Memorize the details," said the captain. "It will be harder in the dark."

The soldier took the binoculars away from his eyes, and the four men stood there without speaking.

"You will carry only hand grenades and pistols so you can move more easily. Your rifles will stay behind."

The sergeant thought of something and was about to speak, but changed his mind.

"You will leave from the back of the kitchen area as soon as the sun sets. You will wait by the roadside shrine until night falls. To reach the ravine you will walk by moonlight. The moon sets at midnight. The plateau is within their firing range. You will have to work fast, so as to finish before daylight. Their men shouldn't see you carrying them."

There was a flash of light from the crater in the distance. One of the soldiers saw it first and raised his hand without speaking and pointed toward it. The captain paused. It was just a small flash of light. Then there was another. It was as if someone were signaling. They all held their breath. It was the captain who finally figured out what it was. The sun had begun to set.

"It's only the glint of the sun on their belt buckles," he said, relieved.

They rode to the roadside shrine. They dismounted and sat down until nightfall. They climbed down to the ravine in the dark, tied the mules, and lay low. It was a warm night. Thousands of tiny creatures swarmed through the darkness in a hum of excitement; twigs and pebbles throbbed beneath the erotic rush. One of the soldiers leaned toward the other and said quietly, "It's the fifteenth of August, the Dormition of the Virgin."

The other man nodded in the dark.

"Back in the village people will be fasting," said the first man.

The sergeant gave them a nudge and signaled for them not to talk.

The first two men were from the same village as one of the men in the crater. The sergeant had been drafted at the same time as the other three, but that was all they had in common. The waxing moon shone faintly, a thin sliver that gradually descended and disappeared behind hill 1 2 3 2. The night grew darker by yet another shade. They set out crawling along the trail on all fours. Some animal let out a yelp high up behind them. A piercing cry. They pinned themselves to the ground and waited, but nothing else was heard.

They reached the foot of the rocks, their armpits drenched, their limbs cold, like reptiles. They came to a halt, keeping their ears cocked for the sounds of the night. The stars made the distance even more awesome. They could almost feel the three bodies lying above them, desolate and resigned in their frightful immobility. And higher still, at the crown of the summit, were the machine guns, squinting with a mean indifference, a menace larger than nature. They consulted.

"We're going up," the sergeant said in a whisper.

Slowly, they began climbing up the face of the rock, the sergeant in the lead. He reached the top and stretched his arm out to the man behind him to help him up. He then crawled farther ahead until he felt something woolen brush against his cheek.

"Here he is," he said, turning to the next man.

He fumbled and groped with his hand until he felt the shape of a man's leg against his palm. The pelvic bone was in rigor as if life had never stirred in it.

He got on his knees and lifted the corpse by the armpits. As he did this, something sprang loose from underneath it. The sergeant had no time for another thought; the explosion shattered the night, and immediately afterward machine guns opened fire on them from the top of the rock. The third man was still there and, as all hell broke loose, he curled himself up into a ball, a mere nothing, neither man nor stone.

After the violence had subsided, amidst the calm that followed, he heard someone whispering something to him.

He found the sergeant fallen crosswise over the corpse he had been trying to lift and the second man writhing and holding his abdomen with both hands. He bent down over him and the wounded man put his hands around his neck.

"Vassilis."

He carried the man hanging onto his neck down to lower ground, their bodies touching so that the wounded man's blood soaked right through his own clothes. He could feel it coagulating on his navel. Ever so softly, he laid him down.

"Ay, Vassilis."

"Don't talk."

"They booby-trapped the dead."

"Don't talk. Don't exert yourself."

"Ay, Vassilis, I'm dying. I'm shot in the belly."

"It's nothing. Don't talk."

"I'm losing blood fast."

"Be strong."

"Vassilis, I'm going."

"It's nothing."

"Ay."

"Don't start feeling sorry. Think of your loved ones."

"Vassilis."

"Think of the village back home."

"Harvest time must be near."

"Yes, just about."

"Where's the sergeant?"

"He's still up there."

"We'll be going away together."

"Don't say that."

"Daylight is taking forever."

"It will be any time now."

"Ay."

He touched the other man's forehead.

"Mother."

His forehead turned cold beneath his touch. He felt like crying. Somehow he found the courage to go up the rock once more. He lifted up the sergeant and carried him down. Then he carried down the other body.

The night was drawing quickly to an end. The rock posed no problems anymore. He went up a fourth time and walked around the rim of the crater. He found the remaining two men. He could not recognize them. He pulled off his belt and passed it around the ankles of one of the two. He took cover behind an outcrop and began pulling, gently. He expected to hear a mine explode and then the machine guns. There was nothing. Then he pulled the other body. Again nothing. He carried them both down.

With antlike persistence, he scurried back and forth to the stream until, finally, he was exhausted. He sat down to catch his breath. There was a stench of butchered flesh about him, and he had just become aware of it. Then a breeze blew up. He knew morning had come. Trembling, he got up and untied the mules. He lined up the corpses along the edge of the stream. He pulled the mules into the water so that their saddles were level with the surface of the water, then loaded two on each mule. There was one corpse left over. He did not know who it was. He brought the third mule up close. He leaned over and took the body in his arms, as though it were a wineskin, and with one final effort hoisted it up onto the saddle. The body, as though some trace of life were still left in it, slid gently over to the other side and fell, head first, into the water.

He screamed hysterically: "For Chrissakes, man."

He got in the water. The body was impossible to lift. First, he pulled it out of the water. He hitched the mules in a row, mounted the first one, moved closer to the bank, bent over sideways, took the body by the hair, and pulled it up to his level. He was dripping wet. He placed it across his thighs as one does some valued possession.

A bird warbled and it was dawn.

Soldiers were emerging from the depths of the earth like rats. They splashed water from their canteens on their faces, had something hot to drink, and vanished again. Someone saw the mules approaching the road shrine and went and told the captain. The captain had heard explosions during the night and was not expecting them. He leaped up with joy. Another ten men or so gathered round him. They stared at the approaching procession. One of them took off his hat and began waving it in the air.

Then they froze.

There he was at the head of the convoy, the dead man on his lap. He sat upright on his mule as he rode toward them. The morning sun made his unexpected cargo appear particularly splendid.

As he rode through their midst, the men stepped back silently. The mules came to a halt by themselves. He looked round at them from his saddle. Having passed beyond the limits of human endurance, he had sunk into a state of total indifference. Someone moved forward to help him, extending his hands until the dead man was placed in his arms. Then the rest of the men got busy unloading the dead. There followed a frantic surge of activity to and fro, as if they were running out of time.

He knew the weight had been removed from his thighs, but the lower half of his body was completely numb. He raised his leg up over the mule in an effort to dismount. His leg obeyed as though it were not his own. Still, he knew there was some difference separating him from the dead man. He jumped down, stiff as wood, with a jolt. He took a couple of steps, unable to control his legs.

He heard the captain calling him. He turned and looked at him. The captain took him by the arm and squeezed him, without saying a word. Someone brought him a canteen filled with tea. Weary, he sat down on a rock. This gave him a sweet feeling of reassurance. There in the open air, the encampment resembled a sanctuary. The soldiers had placed the cadavers in a row and were staring at them silently. He felt the warm liquid sing as it went down his throat. Something stirred inside him. It was his body's irrepressible longing for life. He raised his eyes high above the treetops and looked at the sky.

"It's the Feast of the Fifteenth of August," he thought. "People will be fasting in the village."

He thought next of the man who had his belly blown away. He was sad. But deep inside him, joy had begun to well up; a wild, ineffable joy.

1960

For Angeliki and Iakovos

THE RIVER KÁYSTROS

Thomás first met his wife in the street. It was the last year of the German occupation, and he had a dried-fruit pushcart in front of the ophthalmology clinic. Just one block over, in the basement on the corner of Homerou and Panepistemiou, there was a dressmaker's shop.

Every day, during her noon break, Anna came out to buy pumpkin seeds. Being the youngest in the shop, she had to do the errands for the other girls. She would leave the money on the glass top of the pushcart, and while Thomás was busy weighing the small paper bags, she was busy studying him, unobserved. She would take them and, blushing, leave in a hurry. She was short—but not too short—and slender, around sixteen. Thomás thought about speaking to her, but, in the meantime, the shop closed down and he did not see her again.

Thomás, at the time, was almost twenty-two and had never been with a woman. Damianos Toplidis, a machinist's apprentice, and Elias Bezetakos, a reserve laborer in the Piraeus Port Authority, his two closest friends at that time, were in the habit of going for a long walk on Saturdays: starting from Phyles Street, through Bathes Square, going from bordello to bordello, stopping at the Metaxourgeio Silk Factory district. They had often encouraged him to join them. And even though this walk titillated his imagination, and in spite of the discomfort from his unrequited dreams, which left him exhausted for the rest of the night with unfulfilled sexual yearning, he refused. He insisted that it should only happen when he fell in love.

Lela was a tall blonde with a big dog, which she walked every afternoon. She was a maid in one of the houses on Massalias Street. She often passed in front of Thomás's stand and on occasion she bought things. The way she had of copying her mistress's mannerisms to perfection, plus the dog and the house on Massalias Street, made her unusually glamorous. Thomás began showing her, cautiously, that he liked her, and she, in turn, responded. From then on, regardless of whether she bought anything or not, she would stop for a while and visit with him. One night, in fact, as she was saying good-bye, she called him "my dear." Thomás couldn't believe it. He stood motionless, waves of happiness billowing up inside of him. He continued to watch her until she turned the corner of Sina Street, she walking in front, the dog behind. Mesmerized, he walked to the corner railing and craned his neck, so he could observe her without being seen and catch just one more glimpse of her. He was just in time to see her disappearing down Bessarionos Street, arm in arm with a German soldier. It felt like a ton of bricks had been dumped on him. He left his pushcart where it was and ran after her, his heart at the breaking point. He saw her kiss the German. He was holding her against a garage door, and she was clinging to his neck, the dog's leash around her wrist. After returning to pick up his cart, he walked down to Stadiou Street, crossed Klauthmonos Square, and, until the heavy traffic subsided, pushed it along aimlessly through the deserted commercial avenues. All this in early April. The next day he picked a new spot. He set up shop at the entrance of Zappeion Park, on the side of Amalias Avenue. Anger gnawed at him for a whole week, and he made up his mind he would hate women for as long as he lived. But, gradually, he began to forget. His glands functioned independently of his volition, and they had started to trouble him once more. He would stare at the women passing in front of him, some by themselves, some in pairs, tanned and bare-armed, dazzling him with their scent. He wanted to fall in love again.

Early one Sunday afternoon, he saw Anna. She was standing in front of the Anglican Church and was about to cross the street. Thomás thought she had grown a little taller. He called out to her and she hesitated at first, as if she hadn't recognized him right away. Then she said hello and started blushing. His awkwardness was every bit as bad as hers, but he did not want to miss his chance.

"Where do you work these days?" he asked her.

"I don't work."

"Where are you going?"

"To see an aunt of mine in Metz."

"I was going to the stadium to see the games. Do you want to walk there?"

Anna said nothing. Neither "yes" nor "no." Thomás got behind his cart and began pushing.

There had been a shower earlier, and even though the road surface had dried, the air still carried the freshness of the water. They reached the statue of the discus thrower without speaking. The stadium was empty.

"They must have postponed the games for fear of the rain," Thomás said.

Anna said nothing. They crossed the bridge and stopped by the pillars of the main entrance. The iron gates were shut. This was a genuine hurdle and, at the same time, meant the end. Anna would be leaving any minute now. Thomás tried to think of something that could change this course of events, but his mind was at a standstill. A vague feeling of panic began to sweep over him. He let go of the cart and crossed his arms. The sky over Zappeion Park was ballooning unnaturally.

"Listen," he said to Anna.

She stood there, hunched slightly over and not speaking, as if she were leaving it to him to take the initiative for everything that was about to happen to him.

"I lied to you about the games. I said it so we could walk here together."

"I know," Anna said, and began fidgeting with her hands.

Thomás was embarrassed, but could no longer back down.

"Do you want to meet again?" he asked her. "I won't bring the cart so we can circulate more freely."

She raised her eyes and looked at him for the first time.

"I'm engaged," she said.

Thomás hadn't expected this. He lowered his head, not knowing what to do. He noticed her fidgeting nervously again with her hands.

"With no engagement ring," he said to her.

"We've given our promise. We'll exchange rings next month."

It must have been his destiny. He was beginning to choke with anger again—a bit different this time. Anger because he felt ridiculous, and anger at Anna herself, who had been pledged already yet stood there in front of him as though she were expecting something.

"There's my aunt," she said.

In the brilliance of the aftershower, Thomás could make out a broad-hipped, strong, forty-year-old woman approaching from the direction of the swimming club. She carried a basket of garden greens on her back, and behind her, as in the background of a painting, the most dazzling rainbow was forming between the hills of Philopappos and the Acropolis. It was an apotheosis.

As she crossed the streetcar tracks, she caught sight of the two of them. Without a trace of surprise she changed direction and walked toward them. As she came closer, Thomás was able to see her features more clearly. She was blond and, in spite of the tiny lines around her eyes and lips, her face was youthful, almost like a girl's. She set her basket down, and for a few moments she carefully studied Thomás. But her gaze held neither hostility, curiosity, nor scorn. It was unpretentious, and for this very reason, calming and reassuring.

"Who is the young gentleman?" she asked without taking her eyes off him.

Her question was also without pretension. And although, ostensibly, it was being put to Anna, it was meant for him alone. Anna remained silent.

Thomás introduced himself. And although he had felt like running when Anna first spotted her, he was now feeling emboldened by the decency of her attitude. He told her who he was, but also how much he loved Anna, how intensely he wanted to marry her, how happy he wanted to make her—he alone and no one else. He told her everything straight out, though somewhat garbled, without stopping for breath. He poured out his soul there at her feet, dredging up all the bitter loneliness in his body until he was completely drained.

"Poor lad," she said. And she turned to look at Anna.

That was just like Aunt Matina. The other suitor had come to her for Anna's hand, and it was she who had arranged for them to exchange vows. Now it was she again who would undo it all.

Months later Thomás, by then much more in control of himself, was curious to learn the reason for her change of heart and asked her about it. She replied simply, "I had never heard a declaration of love quite like yours before."

The details were arranged on the spot. In short, the whole affair would have to be presented as an elopement. Not a voluntary elopement, because Aunt Matina did not want anyone to be hurt. Anna needed to disappear for a few days, and when the misgivings of all concerned had been put to rest, she would show up at her aunt's place once more, but this time as a respectable lady, married by a priest and in church, too. Everything else, she would see to it, would be taken care of. It would be up to them, up to Thomás, that is, to show themselves worthy of her love and trust, and to follow her instructions. Her determination scared him. Scared, not intimidated him, which Aunt Matina picked up immediately. So when Thomás tried to mumble some reservations, simple reservations about his unpreparedness for the suddenness of it all, she stopped him with an ultimatum. .

"You either take your filly and get out of my sight, or the other man gets her."

Thomás gave in. He took Anna to his mother's and then set out to find Damianos and Elias.

His mother had been through a lot herself. She was still nursing him when she brought him from Smyrna in 1922, and she had worked hard in order to raise him. The harshness and the loneliness of the life she had led—a loneliness relieved by several clandestine and very short interludes, with fear of discovery wearing her out in advance (and guilt for her infidelity toward a dead husband and a very young son finishing her off)—had left their marks on her. A woman of few words throughout her life, she knew that she had not raised this son to be her own lover, and she also understood, from the vantage point of her own setting sun, that a human life is nothing much. She set all her bitterness aside, less because her own life had been wasted than because that was the way life was, and accepted Anna to the very best of her abilities, without reservations but without much enthusiasm either. One did not need to be terribly experienced to know that the bride her son brought home with him was an inexperienced young woman. Sizing her up, and noticing her narrow pelvis, which was clearly visible under her short, worn cotton dress, she thought: she will have painful childbirths. And she began to like her.

The wedding took place that same evening at the home of the bridegroom, with Damianos as best man and Elias as second groomsman. The priest, who had had a summary ordination typical of the occupation years, had no parish of his own and made his living by sprinkling neighborhood homes with holy water and officiating at Holy Unction ceremonies whenever he was asked. The two tall candlesticks were the most luxurious feature of the wedding. Elias had found them all by himself, on a Sunday and on such short notice, too. They were white, solid, with no ribbons, but with embossed motifs on them. They were used, but who would notice at such a time. Elias had also removed the funereal mauve ribbons, as the candlesticks were supposed to be returned, in their original good condition, after the wedding ceremony.

He had had to walk two kilometers in order to borrow them from the "Mystras" office annex on Petros Rallis Avenue. The fee, following serious haggling, was agreed upon then and there: three gallons of olive oil, payable in advance. Elias never revealed the secret of his success. Because, aside from the necessity of providing the candles, there was also his own macabre inclination for playing practical jokes, which he quickly suppressed for fear of hexing the couple. This fear was completely unfounded as far as the newlyweds were concerned, although Elias never found that out. He was killed by a stray bullet a few months later during the December uprising in Athens, somewhere in the general area of the Silk Works, as he was trying to cross from the ELAS Liberation Army lines over to the other side. He was peddling British cigarettes and other such goods in demand at the time.

Twenty-four years have passed since then. Anna bore Thomás three sons and, contrary to her mother-in-law's predictions, her births were easy. But her mother-in-law did not live long enough to see this. She died at the age of fifty-five, without so much as a sound, for almost no reason. One evening she was helping Anna, who was indisposed, clear the table, and while she was doing the dishes she said to her: "If it's a girl, I want her to have my name." These were her last words. The next morning, curious about her silence, Anna and Thomás found her already dead in her bed. They buried her the following day. For Thomás this was—and would remain—the second turning point in his life, the first being his marriage. There were the births of his children, of course, but these events had the immediacy of natural processes. And since the baptisms took place at later dates, religious ritual did not manage to color those events either.

His first son's godfather was Damianos, in accordance with the dictates of custom: the best man must be the godfather. These commitments and the friendship they presupposed did not stand the test of time. It has been over five years now since Damianos's relations with Thomás and Anna have begun to cool.

Persephone was the cause of it all. Damianos, a sworn bachelor, had been involved with her for about two years. He used to drag her to his friends' homes on holidays, to parties and celebrations, but had no intention of ever marrying her. "Who, her?" he would say. When Persephone became pregnant and refused to have an abortion, he blamed everybody he knew.

Thomás is convinced he will have to come to terms with this. "It's just a matter of time," he keeps saying.

"How much time?" Anna jibes at him.

Anna is not the skinny cricket that she used to be. Childbirth and household chores have made her put on weight. Gone is her old figure. She has become "like a bag," as she says. But even now there are moments when there is something in her gaze, a spark from the old days, something from the good old days when she was in her prime, just a tiny spark. Thomás gets all teary-eyed when he looks at her. For no reason he has become very emotional. They still sleep in the same double bed which, because of their tight budget, he bought from the Monastiraki flea market on the second day of their marriage. It is too small for them now. The fire that made them think this smallness was an advantage has cooled down considerably, but Anna says nothing because she knows Thomás is planning to buy her a new, more expensive, king-size bed, the perfect one for her. And he is really going to do it, one of these days. Forty-five years old, his hair thinning and his waist bulging, Thomás worries excessively about his sons. The eldest is in the service, the second one wants to become a ship's engineer, but Anna won't let him and they fight like crazy about it. And Thomás laughs to himself and wonders who this tough kid has taken after—probably a distant uncle of his who had joined up with the notorious bandit Tsákitzis—full of amazement at the routes family blood will follow before it comes to the surface!

His third and youngest son is his true hope. He is attending high school and will probably achieve all those things he never did or dared to except in his dreams. He's the spitting image of his grandmother, and cut from the same cloth, too. Just as careful with his words as she was, and people who don't waste any words are resolute. At this thought Thomás's mind begins to wander: he thinks next of his mother who brought him at the age of six months from Ionia and, improbable as this sounds, a picture of that place is still half-buried in his consciousness, the courtyard with the grapevine in his father's house on the slopes of Mount Odemesion, the view overlooking the valley of the river Káystros. But how is it possible he would still retain this memory, or was it sucked from her breast? Thomás is unable to find an answer to this and leaves the past behind. He begins to dream of Anna and himself instead, of how the two of them will grow old together, that is. Bittersweet dreams, naturally, and a bit pessimistic, but without the slightest hint of death overshadowing them. At least not yet.

1966

They laid me on a gurney—a stretcher with wheels. Then they removed my clothing. They cut off my pants and my underwear with a scissors so that it wouldn't be too painful for me. The nurse told me they were going to take some X rays. She was still young and quite cheerful. I asked her if that, too, was going to be something of an ordeal. "No," she said. "They won't move you at all."

She went and opened the doors up wide so that we could get through.

The X-ray laboratory was dark, and it took a few minutes for my eyes to get accustomed to it. It had a moldy smell, like stale pine. I could make out the figure of a doctor, clad in a lead apron, preparing the X-ray machine, bending over it in silence. After a while he motioned to the nurse to step back, and a metal arm began moving evenly along the length of my body. I think there must have been other people there in the room. I thought I heard whispering behind me, and I turned my head to see. Then, as though they had been waiting for that exact moment, someone hollered: "Turn it on." It wasn't the doctor. I heard a lever being pulled and immediately afterward I felt the X ray, or at least so to speak I did, penetrating my flesh and my bones.

This was repeated three or four times. They took X rays of my knees, my pelvis, my chest, and my skull. Each time the metal arm moved swiftly and with startling precision to exactly the right spot. The entire procedure took less than three minutes. It was the doctor who finally said, "OK." We were finished. His voice was cold and impassive, as though he were giving an order. There was not a trace of satisfaction in it, no emotion of any kind. I breathed a sigh of relief. A current of air from the open door blew into my face, and the nurse wheeled me back out to the corridor. This time she was pushing me from behind and I was unable to see her. All I could see as she wheeled me, feet first, along that endless corridor, were the bare, shiny walls filing past me.

We ended up in a very poorly lit room with a low ceiling. There was only one window, high up on the far side of the narrow room, barricaded by metal bars and plate glass. Judging by the height of the window and the poor quality of the lighting, I assumed we must have been in some semi-basement area. The nurse moved me to the center of the room, crossed her arms in front of her chest, and stood facing me. I asked her what the next step would be. "They're looking at the X rays," she said. "I think they'll begin surgery in just a few minutes." She still had the same affable expression, but I could nevertheless sense a slight change in her attitude. I was worried that it was perhaps because of all the questions I had been asking.

I stopped and tried to change position, feeling my spine uncomfortably arched on the hard surface of the gurney. I attempted to move, and all of a sudden a searing pain shot from my left hip up to my heart. I bit my lip so as not to scream, and the nurse grabbed hold of both my wrists with one of her hands, as though she were trying to hold me completely still, and placed her other hand on my forehead. "Take it easy!" she said kindly. "You must remain calm, or it won't do you a bit of good." I realized that she was right and I told her so. I could see that in my condition at that moment, any movement at all was not only pointless but could also be harmful. She began stroking my forehead gently, almost maternally. "You must be patient," she continued. "Patience. It's a hard thing to learn, but at times like this it's a lesson we must all put into practice."

I let her continue stroking my forehead; it was making me feel better. I needed to be comforted and she knew it. I am even sure she was aware she had managed to win me over. I asked her for a glass of water. I was thirsty. "I'll bring you one right away," she said. She let go of my wrists, took her hand away from my forehead, and went out of the room. I listened for a minute to the sound of her footsteps in the corridor, until they could no longer be heard.

I was left alone for quite some time. As I waited for her return, in spite of myself, the events of that morning came rushing vividly back to my mind. That air compressor making such a racket; the open sewer holes; the sidewalk with the missing flagstones—that stupid sidewalk; then tripping and fainting and hearing, in my semiconscious state, the ambulance sirens. Why did that have to happen to me? I stifled my impulse to swear out loud and, in an effort to calm the anger fomenting inside my chest, I began looking around at the room.

The walls were painted white, with some awful latex paint. In the far right-hand corner of the room there was a glass cabinet containing surgical instruments; directly above it was an electric clock. I could just make out the second hand moving noiselessly in a perfect circle, but the reflection on the glass cover of the clock prevented me from seeing what time it was. I lifted my wrist so I could look at my own watch and realized at that moment that it was broken and had stopped. Although I am not superstitious, I took that to be a bad omen, and I was overwhelmed by an uncontrollable desire to find out what time it was. As though my very life depended on it. I looked at the window and tried to calculate the time by the light outside. But there was absolutely no change in the light, as though it were frozen high up in that corner, preserved in that thick plate glass. Suddenly, I felt a shiver of fear deep in my guts. I remained quite still and kept my ears cocked in the hope of hearing some kind of noise, any kind, from outside. This was yet another unsettling discovery with immediate repercussions: No sounds from anywhere outside seemed to be reaching this room, and I was engulfed by a sudden wave of panic. At exactly that moment, the nurse came back in. She was, indeed, carrying a glass of water in her hand, but I hadn't heard her coming, and I had a vague suspicion that she had been standing outside the door waiting for quite a while. I think she may have guessed this by the expression on my face.

I saw her bat her eyelids momentarily and look nervously away, but she immediately regained her composure. My face must have been covered by beads of sweat because, without putting down the glass, she reached into her breast pocket, pulled out a scented handkerchief, and began wiping me. After that she tried to give me a drink and she lifted my head up very carefully, like she would a baby's. I refused to drink and I told her that I wasn't thirsty anymore. This didn't seem to bother her at all. She put down the glass in the corner of the room near the door, and came and stood across from me as she had before. All she said to me, rather sadly, was: "You must trust me." And immediately after that, in a completely professional tone of voice: "The doctors are coming."

I could hear their footsteps and the rustle of their gowns as they entered the room. There were two of them, and they stood there over me for some time, with their hands behind their backs, staring silently at me. They were about the same height, a little taller than average, and they must have been about the same age, though it was difficult to tell because they were wearing caps and surgical masks. The only features visible on their faces were their eyes, nothing else. I knew that I had no open wounds anywhere, and seeing their surgeons' outfits was making me feel uneasy. Ignoring the fact that I had insulted her, if you could call my refusal to drink any water an insult, I turned my head to look for the nurse, hoping at least for a nod of encouragement from her. But the nurse was now bending over the glass cabinet with the instruments, and all I could see was her rounded buttocks and a small area of exposed flesh between her deathly white stockings and the hem of her skirt. Then I could no longer see anything at all.

Someone had pulled a switch and the room was suddenly flooded by a harsh, glaring light. I lifted up my hand to shield my eyes, and I could make out the figures of the two men and a third man between them, who immediately disappeared.

It seemed strange to me that at no time before had I been conscious of my nakedness in the presence of the nurse. But now, beneath that blinding light and the doctors' scrutinizing gaze, I realized how exposed and unprotected my body was. "I'm entirely in their hands,"

I thought, trying to rest my head in a more comfortable position on the smooth surface of the table. I turned it back at a slant to try and avoid straining my neck, and through the lashes of my half-closed eyelids I could see one of them, his shoulders tilted slightly back, examining the X rays, still wet from the developing chemicals. He held them against the light for a minute, glanced at them quickly, and then passed them on to the other doctor. Then they put them down somewhere, and the second doctor came over to me, taking hold of my jaw and turning my head so I faced him. It was the same exact way my father used to hold my face when I was a boy, and through some silly kind of association, I half-expected to be given a slap. Instead, with a quick, polished motion, he placed his thumbs at the base of my nose, quickly inverted my eyelids, and examined them from the inside. He released them immediately, and through a multicolored whirl of dark specks of light I heard him say: "We can begin." It was the first and only thing either of them said or would say for quite some time.

By the time I managed to open my eyes again they had already begun working on my legs. The light didn't bother me as much now, and it was possible, with considerable effort, to lift my head and observe what they were doing. They worked quickly and quietly, their movements perfectly synchronized. The nurse had her back to me and was holding my feet completely still at the level of her waist. Her position seemed somewhat unnatural to me; she could just as easily have done the same thing standing in a more normal position. I thought for a moment that she might be trying to avoid my gaze and that worried me somehow. Nevertheless, the fact that until that moment, contrary to my expectations, I had not felt any pain made me take heart. I saw the doctors' hands working deftly and with precision, and in spite of the humiliation I felt because of their behavior toward me, I had to admit that they were very skilled at their job.

They had already wrapped my legs all the way up in plaster—it looked like I was wearing those leggings from World War I—and were proceeding unimpeded further up my body. The memory of that sharp pain in my hip was beginning to make me want to jump out of my skin, and I began thinking that it wouldn't be long before things started getting rough. I held my breath and gritted my teeth so as to bear up under the wave of pain that was about to come, but, strangely, no such thing happened. I felt nothing but the doctors' fingers deftly probing my muscles, followed by the pressure of the tape being wrapped tightly around my skin, and, I must confess, an imperceptible quiver of excitement running up my spine. The doctor must have realized this, because he stopped working for a minute, glanced quickly at me, and whispered something to the other doctor, who listened dispassionately and without expression.

Things started getting difficult up around my hips. Even to me, and I was no expert, it was obvious that in order to continue bandaging me up, if indeed it was necessary to continue, they would have to move me, or at least move me slightly off the table, so that my body was no longer in contact with it. With an almost morbid curiosity, as if all this had little direct bearing on me, I waited to see what would happen next.

The doctors had stopped working and had moved to a corner of the room where they were having a kind of informal consultation. I couldn't see them. I could only see the nurse standing firmly rooted in the same position, still holding my feet against her waist. I studied the curve of her neck and the slope of her shoulders, and I suddenly felt pity for her. My earlier impression that she was young and cheerful was false. She was simply another frightened, downtrodden creature, condemned by some unfathomable volition to perform a job she disliked, and she was trying to do the best she could with whatever remnants of dignity she could still muster up from within. I began to feel an overwhelming sense of regret for having been suspicious of her, and I wanted to tell her about it, but I was stopped by the thought that it was probably forbidden to say such things. I tried to turn my head toward the corner where the doctors had disappeared, but I was unable to see them. I could sense them behind me, huddled in that corner, communicating with each other through gestures and signs. I couldn't even hear any whispering, and it was then that a sudden fear shot through me like a lightning bolt, a fear that the two men behind me were conspiring against me and that they were plotting to do me in. Before I had time to react to my fear, they had already anticipated my reaction, and they hurled themselves upon me. They grabbed my arms and held them in check while a soft yet incredibly strong and sturdy hand was clamped over my mouth. I could feel a wedding band on the inside of the ring finger mashing my lips against my teeth. The pain was unbearable, and through it all I could hear a bench being pulled and the thud of my feet being placed on it. Then I saw the nurse coming toward me with a large needle in her hand. She had a sad, Madonna-like expression. She didn't even have to tie the rubber band around my arm. My veins were already standing out like ropes due to the grip they had on my arms, which were being held immobile. She bent over me carefully, found the right place with no difficulty, and plunged the needle into me. I felt the strange fluid, its temperature different from that of my own body, coursing through my blood, and by the time the contents of the needle had been emptied into me, I was already out cold.

When I came to they had wrapped my entire body in plaster. My belly and my chest protruded upward in a snow-white mound, and the shape of my hips was unnaturally exaggerated. I imagined that I must have looked obese, a bit like a Cycladic idol or maybe an astronaut in his space suit. They had left nothing but my face uncovered, and perhaps because I was no longer dangerous now that I was entirely in their hands, the doctors had removed their masks. One of them was completely bald and he reminded me of someone, but I couldn't quite figure out who. He had stepped back a few paces, as if admiring his work, a smile etched on his face, which was reminiscent of an animal's grimace. I noticed the backward arch of his stance and guessed that he must be suffering from a crooked spine. The other doctor was still stooped over me, sculpting lines in the area between my chest and my navel, a perverse satisfaction apparent in his paranoid gaze. I had a sudden idea that perhaps he was drawing dirty pictures, and I smiled. It was, after all, a perfect surface for an artist to decorate.

When they did address me it was not because they had any inclination whatsoever to explain themselves. Until then they had treated
me like an object, but perhaps on some deeper level they needed their
work to be approved by me as well. The one with the penchant for
sculpting spoke: "It was for your own good," he said. "Our idea...."
        I didn't let him continue. I had finally realized, though too late,
what was going on. I said, "With all due respect for your remarkable
dexterity, I must say I find it impossible to believe that you could have
any ideas whatsoever."
        I suppose they were not expecting my insolence. I saw their
expressions clouded over by a combination of anger and regret in the
face of my ungratefulness. I must confess that although there was
really nothing worse to expect, I was scared. I glanced around looking
for the nurse. She was standing at my head, holding a bowl with the
remaining plaster mixture. She looked at me sadly, with a well-mean-
ing air of reproach and an expression on her face that was patience
incarnate. Before I had time to realize what was about to happen, the
bald-headed man came over to the nurse, took a trowelful of plaster,
and tossed it into my eyes. I felt the burning sensation of the plaster
on my pupils, and at that moment, in a final burst of insight, I remembered who it was he reminded me of. The doctor was the very same
man who had been operating the air compressor. The burning pain
made me want to scream, but I gritted my teeth instead. Then two
strong, viselike fingers took hold of my jawbones and began to pry
them apart until they were forced open. I felt my mouth filling with
the thick, wet mixture of plaster. It had a taste which was not entirely
unpleasant, but by then I had already begun to suffocate.

1970

One of them was standing behind me reading what was supposedly my wife's statement. I didn't even have the courage to protest. I asked them where they were holding her. They answered that she was in good hands. They then asked me again about Wednesday evening. I knew their technique. I told them that I had already answered that question. One of them banged his hand on the table and stood up. The lights were blinding me. I could hardly see them.

"You met with Argyropoulos at Omonoia Square. And then you went for coffee. I want to know what happened then."

"Nothing happened then. We went our separate ways at the Nikoloudi Arcade. I took the streetcar from the academy to go home."

"Argyropoulos's statement is very different."

"It probably is."

"I don't understand why."

"I can't say it any more clearly."

"How long did you stay at the Petrograd?"

"Maybe three-quarters of an hour. Maybe more. After his coffee Michalis ordered a brandy."

"Now there's an earth-shaking piece of information."

"I hadn't seen him for fourteen years. Not since the day of his second trial."

"Just tell us what you talked about."

"Women."

"Don't be such a smart aleck."

"I'm not trying to be a smart aleck."

"How old is your daughter?"

"I don't think that has anything to do with all this. Okay, she's seven."

"Argyropoulos says you were waiting for someone."

"Then Argyropoulos ought to know who it was."

"You would make things easier on yourself if you told us all you know yourself. Ingeborg, whose name was in your address book, has been located in Rhodes."

"I've got nothing to say, unless interrogators like racy stories."

"Interrogators are interested in facts, like four bomb explosions in twelve days. You could make things a lot easier on yourself."

He must have thought I was an idiot, or else he was one.

"I have nothing to tell."

Another man came in at this point. It was the first time I heard his voice.

"Out there, they think of you as a soaring eagle. Don't turn out to be a barnyard rooster."

The comment was calculated to hit two ways, and it was humorous. I thought of telling him that, but all I said was, "Right."

He must have thought my response was sarcastic. He took some time before speaking again. His voice was soft and sharp-edged, like a razor blade.

"I am in a position to shut your mouth forever, or to open it so it never closes again."

I could tell he was seething mad. Up to that point they had been careful not to touch me. That just made things all the more threatening.

"I'll level with you: I suggest you spill everything you know of your own accord."

I couldn't think of anything to say, so I said "right" again. A stream of air brushed past my face as he raised his hand, but before he could bring it down on me the door opened and the lights were dimmed.

Another man had shown up. He was wearing a tie and his shirt-sleeves were rolled up. The smell of soap assaulted my nostrils. He was clean-shaven, and he looked me over as if I were an inanimate object. The other men got up from their chairs. I could tell from their silence that there was a kind of complicity between them.

He told them to take me away. Two men took me by the arms and pushed me outside. A typewriter could be heard from the far end of the corridor. I was taken down to the sub-basement. The cell was dark and the door shut on me like an incinerator door. I stood in the middle of the floor and stretched out my arms, the way arthropods spread out their antennae, trying to touch the walls. The walls were cool and smooth, covered with a thin layer of dust, which stuck to my fingertips. I walked to one corner, leaned my back against the wall, and let my body slide downward.

In the dark I could feel my eyes burning from the interrogation lights and the nerve endings in the back of my eyes still felt like hot coils. I knew they were trying to break me. Feeling drained from lack of sleep and the torment of the interrogation, I turned on my side and pulled up my knees, curling up like a jackknife, feeling crushed beneath the weight of the four-story building above me as though I were under tons of atmospheric pressure.

They woke me up and took me to a different room, which looked like a schoolroom. There were some benches in it, and a blackboard on a stand in the corner. They left me there without saying a word. Through a solitary window some light, real, authentic daylight, was coming in. The window was very high and it probably looked out on a courtyard. As I waited for them to come in, I sat trying to figure out what this whole setup might signify. I then had a sudden urge to look outside that window. I stuck my ear to the door but couldn't hear anything outside. I placed two benches against the wall, climbed up on them, and jumped as high as I could, trying to grab hold of the window ledge. As I was doing this, the benches fell out from under me and my hands just could not hold me up.

Before falling back down I managed to catch a glimpse of the sky, serrated by the tiled roof across the street.

I got up amid the clatter and the dust, afraid I might have broken something, my eyes glued to the door. I heard the key turn, and when the door opened there was a tall man standing there, in uniform and with rank insignia, too. He stood there for some time staring at me grimly. Then he came over to me. "Scum," he said coldly.

I sensed the danger and tried to keep calm, but it only served to provoke him. He raised his leg adeptly and brought down the heel of his boot on my toes. I was wearing a pair of light canvas shoes when I was arrested. The pain went straight to my heart. I bent forward so as not to scream and saw him bending his knee, getting ready to kick me in the groin. My reflexes were fast and I was just in time to pull my hands in front of me to shield myself. This made him even angrier. He tripped, pulled back a couple of steps, and from there, putting all his weight behind him, brought down his fist on my face.

My glasses flew away, and blood started pouring down my face. Half-blinded, I felt him grab me from behind. He took me by the neck like a puppy, shook me a few times, threw me down on my knees, and shoved my face into an ashtray filled with sand, cigarette butts, and wads of spittle. There was no time to feel nauseous as I was expecting that at any moment he would finish me off with a few swift kicks.

Completely unexpectedly, he let go of me. For a while I could hear him panting heavily, out of breath. He called me "scum" once more and went out. I heard the key turn in the door. I stayed in the same place for a long time, lacking the strength to move, feeling a strange sort of satisfaction that things had not gone any further. I found my glasses and put them on. I got up and wiped my hands on my pants. I was wondering if the whole incident was part of the ritual of the interrogation, or merely my punishment for being bad. I walked over to the blackboard. This must have been the room for the illiterates in the corps. Half-erased letters were still visible on the shiny black surface. I recognized the smell of chalk, even though my nose was still bleeding. I turned around, sat down on a bench, and tilted my head back, trying to get the bleeding to stop. I had not had a nosebleed since childhood. Propped up against the wall, with my head back, I could see the bright square made by the window facing me.

I suddenly heard the voices of people coming downstairs. They were having an argument of some sort in sharp tones. I thought that maybe they were interrogating someone. I immediately thought of Argyropoulos. I listened closely for some time. The words reaching me were indistinct. It was mostly the interrogator's voice I heard. Intrigued, I went over to the window, but still could not make out anything. I went back to my bench. Then the terrible sounds of someone being beaten could suddenly be heard up above. And immediately afterward, they began noisily raising and lowering the blinds. This lasted for a long time. The noise of the blinds was not sufficient to cover the racket being made by the beating. Then, abruptly, a woman's shriek rang out. It began like an animal's howl, and for the longest time it reverberated inside the walls of the courtyard, helpless and desolate. Then, just as abruptly, it stopped, just short of covering the entire gamut of pain. As if a hand had gagged the victim. They were torturing a woman. A second, male scream rang out. Much shorter, almost like a gasp of surprise. I could hear someone swear. "Bitch." I could tell that the tortured woman had bit him. Then windows began to shatter. Someone yelled: "She's gone crazy, hold her down." Then someone else, sounding scared, yelled: "Mrs. D., Mrs. D." It was my wife's name. Even before I had time to take it all in, it was as if I had already witnessed the scene that followed: the man who had been bitten lunging at her, enraged, and finishing her off with a final blow. There followed an interval of silence; then someone made a hurried telephone call requesting an ambulance. They had killed her.

I wanted to restrain myself, but I just couldn't. I started running in circles around the benches. I stopped under the window. I didn't want to give them the satisfaction, but I couldn't help myself. I cupped my hands in front of my mouth and began shouting at the top of my lungs: "Murderers."

The ambulance siren screeched like an echo to my cry. I heard it brake at the front gate. I heard steps on the stairs. They went past me, then went upstairs. My senses were heightened unnaturally. I heard them whispering conspiratorially. I heard the words "cardiac arrest." I heard another voice scolding someone: "That's not how you beat people, moron." Then another set of steps struggling down the stairs. I threw myself against the door and began pounding on it. Someone came running and opened it. He managed to put his leg in front of me and block my way. I was beaten until I collapsed. I began to sob. Out of shame at my own impotence. In tears, I asked the man to see if the woman they were bringing down was alive. I told him she was my wife. He answered that no one was being brought down.

I was sure he was lying to me. I went back and sat on my bench. There was nothing else to do. I began crying softly, almost calmly. The guard got worried. He came over to me and said kindly that he understood and that I should not worry. I raised my eyes and gave him a blank look. I think that I was beginning to come around. He went away and left the door open. He came back after a while with someone in civilian clothes. It was the commandant of the section, and he tried to persuade me that no one had been tortured. I told him calmly that there wasn't a single real man among them. He accepted this without getting angry. He led me to his office saying that he would make a telephone call and have my wife brought to me. He called an orderly and gave instructions to escort me to the wash area.

I had not forgotten the sound of water. I turned the faucet and let it run for a while. Then I washed the blood off my face. They marched me back to the commandant's office. Trying to be polite, he motioned me to a chair.

"Your wife is on the way," he said. "You are only allowed to see her, nothing else. I am not the proper authority for anything more than that."

I said nothing, and this must have made things difficult for him. He went over to the window and looked outside. There were two small ceramic flowerpots with peppers growing in them on the windowsill.

I could feel the water drying up on the back of my neck. Then there was a knock on the door, and the same orderly stuck his head inside.

"The lady is here," he said.

The base commandant motioned him to get out of the way. He stepped aside without speaking. At the end of the corridor, between several other open doors, I caught sight of my wife. She was flanked by two men, as though they had been keeping her there in the wings for some time, ready for the performance. She smiled at me and slowly raised her hand in greeting. Then they took her away. I felt no emotion of any kind. My mind was merely recording things. The commandant went and closed the door himself. He did not comment on my mistaken impression. He simply said, "I'm sorry."

He must have been smart once. He went to the window, cut two leaves from the plants, and rubbed them between his fingers. Then he smelled them. My gaze followed his movements. He sensed it. There he was, all of him, in that one gesture. A resigned, middle-aged man, probably with weight problems. He made an attempt to smile.

"Peppers. I take care of them myself. They remind me of the country."

For a fleeting moment I thought about returning his civility. I thought of telling him that as soon as I got out of there I would cultivate gorse. But I decided the metaphor was somewhat pompous, even if his knowledge of mythology was not that limited. It would make no sense to ruin his mood. In the final analysis, there was something quite human about his hobby and his homesickness for the place he came from. He had not spoken of his "village," he said "the country."

I allowed myself to return his smile.

He stood there uneasily for a moment and then rang the bell for me to be taken away. Two shiny-faced young men came to get me. They took me directly to the room where I had been interrogated. The interrogators were still there waiting for me.

1971

He was born in Kynouria, in the village of Karatoula. He was drafted in 1919. In the fall of 1920, after a year's delay, he was called up for duty in the army.

He reported for duty at Nafplion, right after the November elections—the elections that Venizelos lost—in the regiment of the Eighth Infantry Battalion. They kept him there for three months, taught him to use a machine gun, and sent him off, via Piraeus, to fight in Asia Minor.

There, between March and July of 1920, he took part in the fighting in Eski Sehir—and was decorated for it.

(The victorious Commander Konstantinos himself, "son of the Eagle," paused before him in ancient Dorylaion and pinned the medal on his chest.)

Two weeks later, at the age of twenty-three, during army maneuvers leading up to the decisive attack, he went across the Salt Desert; on an all-day, all-night, stinking, sweat-filled trek, with no water but with excellent morale, all the way to Gordion. They were heading for the "Red Apple Tree" in the Turkish heartland.

When the front collapsed, in 1922, miles and miles away from the Sangarios River, in Ali Veran, he was taken prisoner along with General Trikoupis and the rest of the men from the Third Army Corps.

It was their final battle.

At the Ousak prison camp the survival rate was one out of three and, after hammering rocks down to gravel for eighteen months, he found his way to Cilicia.

During the exchange of 1924, altogether unexpectedly, he was taken down to Smyrna with about three hundred other men.

A Red Cross committee was waiting for them at the station at Basma Hane, and they were gathered en masse and loaded onto a steamship, the *Marika Toyia*, which was leaving from the Iron Steps of Pounta. As it set sail Panayotis, standing on the highest deck, watched the land behind him grow smaller.

Despite all the humiliation he had been through and despite the rags he was covered in, he continued to have an angelic quality about him.

It was much later that his illness first appeared, at the end of 1927. His right hand began to shake, it was something like Parkinson's disease. He also began to stutter. The doctors who examined him were of the opinion that it was due to the hardships of captivity.

An old war buddy of his, a party boss, urged him to apply for a pension. He helped him to fill out the papers. They sent them to the ministry and waited. Nine months later he received a negative answer.

In the meantime, his mother died and so did an older brother of his who had been supporting them both.

For a long time, to make ends meet, Panayotis ran errands for people. Then he was forced to start begging, which he did in his own peculiar way; he would gather dried herbs, like oregano or sage, and sell them, in minute quantities—just a pretext for maintaining whatever pride he still had left.

A seamstress from his neighborhood, a onetime childhood sweetheart of his, now married, felt sorry for him and sewed him up a set of calico bags, with pleats at the top. He would fill them patiently, load them on his back, and walk the streets with them. That was how he became known to practically everyone in the Peloponnesus: Panayotis.

Sometimes on the highways, in the heat of summer, some wise-guy truck drivers would stop and pick him up, let him ride next to them, and say the most awful things to him—just to have some fun during their trip.

Even the bums in the small towns where he stayed overnight
would make fun of him. Sometimes they tied cans on him and sometimes bits of paper that they would set on fire.

He accepted it all, not like someone resigned to his fate, but
good-naturedly. Perhaps deep down he, too, enjoyed it.

In 1957, on my way down from Macedonia, while on furlough,
I ran into him in Argos, at a brothel. Trying to sell fertility herbs to the
women. We were distant relatives through marriage, and when he saw
me he turned red with embarrassment. He must have been almost
sixty then. In 1973 he retired permanently to his village. He was old
by then, he was losing his eyesight, and his legs were no longer strong
enough to carry him around like they used to. Some nieces of his took
him in. They gave him his meals and one of them laundered his only
change of clothing for him every other week. In return, he would take
the two or three goats they kept in their cellar out to pasture.

He died that same year, in the month of August. He had taken
the animals out to graze, felt thirsty, and bent down to drink from
some water hole, lost his balance, and drowned—in only four
inches of water.

1977

THE STEPFATHER

A long time ago, when my stepfather was a boy, he came down with
the mumps. In spite of the fact that his folks had taken the precaution
of applying a small amount of tar ointment behind his ears and tying
some goatskin cord around his waist the minute the first symptoms
appeared. Their home remedies had no effect. The disease spread like
wildfire down through his body, until it reached his private parts,
which swelled up so badly they were of no use to him forever after.

In a small, closed community like our village in those days, it was
difficult to hide a thing like that. So, when my stepfather reached adolescence and began chasing girls, they would avoid him, having been
warned by their mothers that they would never be able to have children by him. One would think that such an unfortunate stroke of luck
would have had a bad effect on his character. That it would have made
him small-minded, arrogant, stingy, or mean, but it did nothing of the
sort. Quite the opposite, in fact, it brought out his positive qualities,
which became even stronger with the passage of time, and resulted in
his adopting an outlook on life that was both easygoing and sensible.

When our ma was widowed, at the age of thirty-two, he was
almost forty. And as soon as the yearlong mourning period was over
he went, by himself, to pay a visit to her mother-in-law, or rather our
grandma, our real father's ma, and asked her to hear him out.

"I have a steady job," he said to her. "I can't have kids and I want
to marry Maritsa."

I remember Grandma only vaguely, but she must have been a
strong woman. She had also been widowed young and left with four
children, so she tried to pressure Ma into it, but Ma, still clinging to
some outdated moral code, wouldn't hear a word of it. In the end,
Grandma did get her to agree to the marriage.

Our stepfather was a barrel-maker. Every summer, round the middle of August, he threw all his tools in a big satchel and went down to the plain of Mantineia to work. He would stay there until harvest time, repairing old barrels. He did minor repairs, replacing rotten barrelheads, broken staves, stuff like that. Then, at summer's end, he would come back to the village.

We were too young to know much about seasons, but we could tell when it was getting near time to see him again by Ma's working herself up into a bustle of activity, which would manifest itself by her cleaning the house in a state of frenzy for almost a week before. She would sweep the yard, whitewash the stone wall, and work her hands to the bone scrubbing the floors and polishing them with leaves from the walnut tree. On the last day she seemed to slow down a little bit. She would get up in the morning, make dough, cover the bread, and let it stand, and while it soundlessly and unhurriedly rose, she would bathe us, give us a soggy piece of bread sprinkled with sugar, and send us off to wait for him at Plakes.

If my memory serves me right, I must have made that trip four or five times. But you'd think all those trips were exactly the same, because in my mind they've all become one. Dinos would walk in front holding Olga by the hand, and Vlassis and I would follow. Plakes was situated about a thousand meters above our house, a boundary we had never, ever crossed. It got its name because in the old days it used to be a Turkish cemetery, and there were still a few "plaque"-shaped gravestones there, sticking straight up out of the ground. Farther back, the rest of the village spread out behind us.

When we got to the top, in the calm height of day, the four of us would sit in a row, without speaking at first, looking down over the mule path, which disappeared from view farther down the slope. It was up this path that our "father" would be coming.

Except for Olga, who was the youngest child, the rest of us knew that he wasn't our real father. But he still slept in the same bed with our ma, bought us shoes twice a year, and carted us to the doctor's when we weren't feeling well. Anyway, we would sit and wait for him. He almost always showed up late. By which time we kids, teary-eyed from the strain of waiting, had begun to play. Every time he came the same thing happened, and we would already have forgotten why we had come up there in the first place when, suddenly, we would hear his booming voice.

"Okay, you kids. Caught you in the act!"

We would turn around, startled, as if some giant had come striding over the mountaintops, and see him a short distance away, standing like some towering Zeus, his bag of tools lying beside him.

He seemed quite amused by our sheepishness, and when Olga, the most innocent of the lot, finally went running over to him, he would let out a resounding laugh, get down on his hands and knees, and start chasing her, barking like a dog. In this way, he was slowly reincarnated, right before our eyes. Then we would all join in the fun and games, until he stopped, exhausted and out of breath. He would get up, adjust his belt, and say, "We'd better get going now. Your ma will kill us."

He would take hold of Olga, who had usually wet her pants by then, under her arms—she died later on of measles, at the age of eleven—and sit her up on his shoulder, take his toolbag in his other hand, and off we would go.

Our entrance into the village was a genuine triumphal procession. Everyone we met along the way wanted to greet our stepfather, and we would stop in almost every yard. As if he had been away in some foreign country for many, many years. I don't know if everyone really liked him, but they all insisted on offering him something to drink and exchanging a few words with him. Words which, when you come right down to it, were just a pretext for the need for some plain old human contact.

When, at last, we would arrive at our house, Ma, who had been waiting all that time, her arms crossed, on the veranda, would quickly turn her back and go inside, which was her way of showing her express disapproval of our inexcusable tardiness.

At that crucial moment, our stepfather would stop short, put Olga down, wink at us, and repeat in a serious tone of voice, "She'll kill us, she's mad as can be."

We would make believe that he was telling us the truth, because we liked the way he put himself in our place and acted like we were all defenseless creatures at her mercy.

We would sneak into our yard like bandits in cahoots, the oven door open and the oven still hot, and as we climbed the stairs, the clatter of plates and silverware as she set the table growing louder and louder, he would stand on his toes, raise his head up, sniff the air and lean backward, and whisper confidentially to us, "But first she'll feed us."

As a rule, the meals we had on the occasion of his return were simple, ritual-like meals, almost like a ceremony. They always consisted of a rooster, which had been slain the previous day—and made tastier by draining its blood during the night—freshly baked barley bread, and wine.

During the meal our stepfather, his sleeves rolled up and the veins standing out on his suntanned hands, would tell us about his trip. It was all just unimportant little things, but the tone of his voice and the way he had of making us see things through his eyes made his tales strangely fascinating. We would listen and Ma—whom he liked to call the Mrs. or the sultana, depending on the moment, whenever he wanted to annoy her, and who, during the thirty-six years that she lived with him, never once let herself show how much she loved him—would wait, with the look of a martyr for whom getting remarried had been some great sacrifice, for him to finish the last glass of wine, then wash and put away the dishes, close the shutters of their bedroom, and send us out to play, because "Father" was tired and had to get some sleep.

We knew there was no arguing with her. We would rise obediently, Dinos and Olga first, then Vlassis and finally me, and go out to the yard. Her impatience to get rid of us, as well as the strange, almost unnatural silence that shrouded the house behind us, was something we were not yet able to comprehend.

Eventually, after quite some time, as the afternoon sun was beginning to set, the window shutters above us would again be opened up. We could see Ma standing between them, peering out at us with a look of appeasement on her face but nevertheless glaring at us in her usual stern way. Then she would disappear, and we could hear her in the kitchen struggling with the pots and pans. This was our signal that life would once again be continuing as usual until the following August.

All these memories, mixed with the smell of planed wood and caulk that our stepfather brought home from his barrel-making on the plain of Mantineia, continue to flow, riverlike, through my mind.

Many years later I was working as an agronomist in Doxato, Drama. In 1964, the night before Ascension Day, I received an urgent telegram from my village.

"Father ill."

I realized it was the end. I asked for five days' leave and took the train down to Tripoli. From there I continued by taxi. The mule path was no longer there, nor were the Plakes. The bulldozers had made short work of them.

I got there just before the old man passed away. He had fallen into a coma and the end was rather peaceful. We buried him the following day. Dinos, who was a tax collector in Skiathos, had hired a boat and arrived at the last minute.

"Remember to go find our Vlassis," our ma cried out wildly as they were lowering the body into the grave.

She was a wreck, and between her age, her cataracts, and her sleepless nights, she could barely stay on her feet. She may also have been thinking at that moment about her first husband, our father, I don't know. At any rate, "our" brother Vlassis had been killed in 1948, during the Battle of Mourgana, and had been buried in some unknown place, without any graveside offerings from his family.

Poor old Ma.

As soon as the last shovelful of dirt had been thrown in, Dinos and I took her by the arms and went back to the house. She refused to lie down, and while two of her nieces prepared coffee for the condolence callers, she sat in a corner, stiff-bodied, close-mouthed, and dry-eyed. There was nothing that could attract her attention once that process of hardening her face into a mask had begun.

Now that she was alone, Dinos and I should have talked about her future. We postponed it for later. I couldn't stand seeing her like that anymore, so I got up and went out on the balcony. I leaned my elbows on the banister—he had made it himself from a chestnut tree. I could hear the noisy din of chitchat coming from inside, as the folks who had come to pay their last respects tried, through their small talk, to ward off their panic.

"This wood is strong as the devil. You can leave it out anywhere, rain or shine. It may split, or become discolored, but it will never rot."

It's funny but I only realized how short our giant had been—under five feet four inches—the previous night when the women, after having washed and changed him, called me in to help lay him in his coffin.

1977

AUTUMN STORM

My husband was arrested on the first day of the "revolution"—to be exact, on the first night of the revolution—and has been in detention on the island of Leros ever since. This, his third arrest in a row, was purely "preventive" in nature and, precisely for this reason, totally meaningless. He had been employed up to that time by various publications as a crossword puzzle composer, and a crossword puzzle composer simply cannot be considered dangerous in any serious way. I may be the only one who calls him a composer, in jest of course. He prefers the term "constructor," which is more consistent with his views concerning creativity, and also with his strict sense of order—an outlook he has faithfully adhered to since his childhood. He learned this trade during the long years he spent in different prisons, so he wouldn't lose his mind, or so he says. As far as I am concerned, the fact that he chose this particular way to maintain his sanity, in light of the enormous self-discipline political prisoners need when faced with the loss of liberty, suggests something else, which he would have a hard time admitting: a creeping sense of insecurity as far back as that time. I did not know him during his two prior detentions. It was only afterward that we met, in 1963, toward the end of September, at the opening of the wine festival in Daphní. He had just been released from jail under the Pacification Act of that year, and had already served four years of the initial sentence, which, according to Statute 509, was to be life.

In spite of the martyr's aura about him and his pale skin, I don't believe I was ever really in love with him. Our marriage was the product of well-thought-out decisions, and our marital relations were based primarily on mutual respect. He was in his late forties and was looking for the few tangibles that he had missed out on, like the feel of a fresh-ironed shirt—another thing he would never admit to. And I was a rather carefree soul, about to turn thirty-three. Ours was not a compromise born of necessity, nor did it prevent us from reaching, at times, states bordering on enthusiasm.

I have been living alone for a little over a year and a half. I am thirty-eight years old, and I work as a language and literature teacher in a private school. A few days ago, totally by chance, I ran into an old lover of mine. I just wrote "totally by chance" without being sure that I did not unconsciously seek this meeting.

I have two daughters of nursery-school age, and even though I am raising them rather strictly, at night, when some fear or other disturbs their sleep, they often climb into bed with me; especially the elder one, who's five, and then the younger one—the three-and-a-half-year-old—follows suit. At such moments, the nearness of their breath and the touch of their skin makes my husbandless year and a half particularly hard to bear.

By nature, I hate kidding myself. I know only too well that that gentle feeling so sweetly and innocently fanning out inside my thighs will eventually awaken the deep and pressing need of my whole being for a good, impersonal, uninhibited fuck.

My reservations, therefore, about the fortuitousness of our encounter go hand and hand with the question: Why him and not some stranger whom I could just as easily have chosen myself? I must tell you that when I was a student I used this approach—with all due discretion of course—most successfully, thus claiming a stake in the approaching women's liberation movement, which, after some delay, has finally reached our country during the last ten years. I should also fill you in on a few details about my old lover. He was both excessive and unfaithful. Our relationship lasted approximately two years. By "approximately" I mean a period of three months of vacillation on my part followed by the decision, again on my part only, to break it off. It had gone too far. It was impossible to take his shallowness anymore. I had come to the conclusion that his infidelities were little more than an expression of his irrational fear of responsibility. It was immaturity pure and simple. When he sensed the danger, he insisted we discuss the possibility of our getting married. Of course, that was not what the whole thing was about. "Settling down" was the last thing on my mind, and I believe that his offer was clearly a defensive move, an effort to create a sense of obligation for himself and, of course, to buy himself some time.

When I told him that my parents had not divorced because of my existence and that, to put it simply, I did not wish to repeat their experience with some child that he might eventually dump on me, he didn't know what to think. He became even more confused when he realized that my decision was final. He broke down. He did not even attempt to do anything about it. Or, rather, he did the only thing that could bring any results; he threw himself on my mercy. And the knowledge that I was getting revenge made me even more uncompromising.

We finally separated. Amicably, without any scenes or entreaties, from him I mean. On this point I want to be fair. Few things are more heartrending than unacknowledged male despair.

At any rate, that first meeting of ours was followed by a second one. This time it was arranged. I had not seen him since 1954. He had not changed much nor had he put on weight or developed the spread around the middle that disfigures men over forty.

We sat at the Aigle Café, in the Zappeion Park. The place was quiet and out of the way. He had picked it. It's funny, though. I had shared so many things with him, so many nights, and yet I felt nervous and even a little bit awkward. As though I was with some stranger. I think he was just as uncomfortable as I was. He told me he was still single. I did not ask him why, and I tried to change the subject. He kept right on though. I knew how persistent he could be and was beginning to suspect where our conversation was leading. Just as I knew exactly what he was trying to conceal beneath that tone of irony he so often had in his voice. He said that the only woman he ever wanted to marry had left him. And that was me.

Was it me he was mocking or himself? It doesn't really matter, but pain should not be made light of. I told him to stop. I became angry and did not want our conversation to continue in that vein.

There was a danger of being caught in the trap of nostalgia. For my part, I knew very well what I was after and I told him what it was in no uncertain terms. In essence, I proposed that we start going out again with no strings attached—free of obligations. He looked at me silently, seeming not to comprehend. Then he asked me if I was sure I wasn't trying to turn back the hands of the clock. His question surprised me. I thought for a moment that he no longer cared for me as a woman. The next moment I felt deeply hurt. Even more deeply than during the years of his infidelities. But he had meant something else. Fourteen years was too long a time to squeeze into a mere parody of our story. The hands of the clock could not be turned back for the simple reason that they had never moved forward. They had stopped at a specific point, and the only thing that could be done was for them to start moving again right where they had left off.

He was certainly not paranoid, and it is equally certain that my five years of married life were a complete blank to him. I, too, of course, would need to blot them out. I stopped and stared at him in amazement. No, he had not changed one bit. He was impetuous as always and, even if we had still been together, he would have been just as unfaithful as he was then.

For a moment I felt a dizzying pull at the thought of a new beginning. Time expands when you're living intensely, but it always ends up as small, compressed cores of memory.

We had spent our only vacation together on one of the islands in the Cyclades. We both enjoyed making love in the open air. I still do. In those days the parched Aegean islands were not overrun by summer hordes. We had left the imprint of our lovemaking all over the island, and I still carry within me those windy, sun-blasted places. But that is all it was. It is not the fact that I have a husband in prison that is holding me back, nor is it my two daughters. I am not puritanical, and I don't think I'm lacking in courage. But a love affair has a fixed duration, and this is one thing, whereas the memories that we carry around with us are quite another. I do acknowledge my loneliness and I know what I need in order to deal with it effectively. Instead, I meet some-

one who is ready to offer me what I had refused once before. I hope I
am not deceiving myself here. Because there is something else I should
tell you—one of those thoughts I have every so often that are so shat-
tering to my sense of certainty: If all I needed was a good fuck, why
didn't I, in fact, seek it with some stranger? Was it fear that my col-
lege-day tactics would prove ineffective at thirty-eight? But suppose I
did not just want a good fuck? We have so many ways to delude ourselves. So why didn't I respond to his proposition? Why was I put off?
Was it because his long-accumulated passion now seemed nothing
more than the sick and prolonged reaction of his wounded ego? Or
was it the realization, at some deeper level, that such things must be
put in their proper perspective? This thought, which is in itself an
admission of the extent of my resignation, is absolutely chilling.

There could also be room here for another interpretation.
Which is that his enduring passion flatters me beyond words. A
reunion according to the dictates of this passion would afford it, if
only temporarily, a modicum of relief. My hard-heartedness—which
this time is working to my disadvantage—lies in my wishing that his
passion will be there forever.

Dear Madam: As you can see, I avoid mentioning your name,
which, in any event, is nothing more than a mask. I have often wished
that I was one of your numerous naive women readers, whose letters
to your column I peruse with such great interest. If that were the
case, I would ask for your advice, shielding myself, of course, behind
an appropriate pen name, such as *Autumn Storm*. I can easily imagine
the liberating power of simple feelings. Unfortunately, though, the
age of innocence is behind me. Still, here I am writing to you. My
reason? To me you are—or you could become—the audience I need
for a story that otherwise could not be made public. I am taking
advantage, therefore, of this possibility.

With warmest regards,

Autumn Storm, at last.

1982

PETER AND PAT

"No, Niko, we have no complaints. You know how we left Greece. Kalliope was still wearing that u.n. Relief Agency coat, even though it was too tight under the arms, and me with my feet full of cuts from walking around barefoot, a seventeen-year-old girl who had never even left her village before. We left on the day of the Epiphany, as they were throwing the cross into the sea at Piraeus. And when we arrived here it was so hot the grasshoppers were all out croaking. Twenty-seven days at sea on the ss *Patris*, I ticked them off one by one. The year before last we read that they had dismantled it—it was the year before last, wasn't it, husband? They had a photograph of it in the *Keryx*, like they do on the obituary page, and it said that they were selling it off piece by piece, after all the Greeks it had transported. I actually started crying, Niko. Because it isn't just what we went through back then, it's that there will be no one around to tell our story; we're the only ones who know, in our hearts, what it was like. Here I was halfway round the world, not speaking the language, getting up in the morning and going off to the factory and waiting for Peter at night so I could talk to someone a little bit before I went crazy, then making him his dinner and preparing some hot, soapy water for his feet, and then, most of the time, he'd just fall asleep in his chair. And the people over here, you should see the way they looked at us, how they looked down on us. And Ilias, once when he was on the bus on his way to see us, they grabbed his newspaper from him, just like that, because he was reading Greek, and Ilias didn't say a word. What could he say, he knew they were doing it to insult him, so what could he do, he got off at the next stop. And to think that Ilias used to fight under Katsareas all over Malevo and Mani. Now we're okay. We have our house, the children are grown up, and we have the other house in Marrickville, but so many years have gone by, and here we are, old and gray, Niko."

"We sure are, woman, we lived our lives and now we're old."

"Yes we did, I must say."

"And Kalliope, Panayiota, do you see her?"

"Oh, Kalliope, you should see Kalliope. We thought we were smart; as soon as we got here, we started working in the factory to escape the slavery of working in muddy fields, and we got stuck there, living off our salaries. She married that shepherd, and in those days you could buy a farm for next to nothing, they were begging to sell. Manolis didn't even know how to sign his name then, and today he's about to make Vassilis a congressman in Adelaide."

"That's not how congressmen are made, woman."

"Yes it is, Peter, that's how they got their farms and all the rest. Property, Niko, Kalliope has tons of it. She hops in that car of hers and it takes her a day to drive around all their land."

"Kalliope?"

"Yes, Kalliope. She worked like a dog for two years. Manolis kept getting laid off; he went from job to job; he was just no good with his hands, poor guy. Anyway, it wasn't long before she became the man, and she just took him and went off, without so much as a backward glance. We were sure that that would be the end of them out there in the wilderness. And she was still nursing her second baby at the time."

"And their children, Panayiota?"

"They married off their daughter last year. And what a fancy wedding it was, with waiters dressed in white and fireworks so bright you could see them all over Australia. Now they're busy with their eldest son, the one I just told you about. He's a fine young man and he's going places."

"All the Greek children are fine youngsters, woman, all of them."

"We certainly did keep them in the fold, if I do say so myself."

"You can say that again."

"From every household at least one child will go on to study. And sometimes two or three. Our younger son is studying to be an accountant, Chrisoula's son Vlassis to be a lawyer, Angelako's Laura is in teachers' college—and there are so many others."

"Our poor children, born in the land of the kangaroos."

"And how about you, now that the children are grown, Panayiota?"

"It's too late for us."

"Do you ever think about coming back to Greece?"

"Oh, Niko, what's there to think about, how can we possibly think about that?"

"What do you mean, woman? If they really do lower the age for retirement to sixty, which they're talking about doing. If they do that—and even if they don't."

"Don't listen to your friend, Niko. We spent one summer there and we'll go again for another summer; that's it and he knows it."

"Oh, come on, now, woman."

"That's the way it is, husband. That's what happens to all of us, Niko. Until you're twenty, you ache and pine for Greece. As soon as you hit twenty, that's it, you don't even realize it. I'd send my kids off to school and my mind would still be over there, thinking about how I used to go out in the fields with my pickax to dig up wild onion bulbs. That's all I needed, to be missing my pickax and those fields. I used to cry so much the doctor at that factory put me on all sorts of pills. In the beginning, everyone took them. Marianthe is still taking them, she has been all her life. Five, ten, fifteen years. In the end, you forget, you give in. I've got white hair now and I'm called Pat and your friend is called Peter, we never even realized it was happening. Twenty, twenty-five years. In a few weeks, on Shrove Monday, it will be our thirty-second anniversary. Can you imagine Shrove Monday in the middle of summer?"

Panayiota stopped talking and gazed calmly but intently at the center of the table. As Panayiota, no matter how long it had been since those cuts on her bare feet had healed, she still felt the pain, but as Pat she had become stoical. She had accepted her routine and would stick to it. The shrimp on the round platter had been finished for quite some time. Big, tasty shrimp from the South Pacific—but not as good as Mediterranean shrimp. And their youngest daughter-in-law had excused herself. She must have been bored to tears.

"Good-night, uncle."

"The poor child can actually speak some Greek," Panayiota commented as she left the room.

The house had wall-to-wall carpeting—the proof of a standard of living of which they were both very proud. It filtered out the noise from the flow of traffic on the nearby highway—noise that was just beginning to die down. It was midnight, and suddenly those fifteen, twenty, twenty-five years, which had gone by so quietly, lost all their sound—and ceased entirely to be heard.

Takis picked up the bottle and filled our glasses up with wine.

"You drive," Panayiota said calmly.

"Oh, all right, woman, I'll drive," he said angrily.

We went out into the yard. The night was humid and there were no stars in the sky. Panayiota stood in the doorway looking at us. Takis put on his safety belt and waited for me to do the same.

"If they stop you, you pay a forty-dollar fine," he said.

He drove slowly and carefully. I felt the moist, warm air float in through the window and stick to my neck.

"That's what our summers are like," Takis said again. "It's going to rain."

We drove on for a while without conversing. Our cheerfulness after the wine—well, you couldn't exactly call it cheerfulness, but whatever it had been at first, it had now given way to melancholy and silence.

I had not seen Takis for thirty-two years. He had been here for thirty-two whole years, on the other side of the globe. For twenty-four of those years he had worked in the same factory. He was getting paid the highest weekly salary, $380 take-home pay. He was a "foreman," respected by the bosses for his accomplishments, and he had earned the privilege of ignoring the time clock if he needed to. Like, for example, when he'd get a phone call that something was going on at home, even some minor problem, I mean, and even if the phone call was just an excuse for him to get away. He had been back to Greece once, and although he insisted that as soon as he retired he would return there, it was certain that he would remain here—permanently.

I gave him a cigarette from my last pack of Greek cigarettes. He took a puff as though he were inhaling nothing but air.

"Our cigarettes over here are much stronger," he said. "They smell like those heavy French cigarettes."

He fell silent once again.

Takis was really someone in our neighborhood, and now he's just plain Peter. He was four years older than I was—which was a big difference in age for us then. It was he, from his chronologically superior vantage point, who first taught me about jerking off—and I still owe that to him. It was a time when my body had suddenly fallen under the power of a blind and baffling turmoil. In addition to the deepening of my voice and my darkening pubis, my chest was aflame, my nipples swollen and so hard that I couldn't even bear the touch of a T-shirt on them. That fever lasted a whole summer.

It was Takis, already seasoned in such matters for some time, who opened my eyes. He was a wild, disobedient youth; he put his old man through absolute hell, and until the time he went into the army he was still waving the rebellious banner of adolescence. Then he got discharged and then he left the country.

I hadn't seen him since then, and now, in the place of my buddy, I had found a middle-aged man getting on in years. Well-disciplined, with a sagging chin and his right eyelid drooping slightly—especially when he had too much to drink—counting the years until his retirement. I wondered how changed I must have seemed to him and if his heart, too, was filled with sadness.

At the hotel, before separating, he gave me a hug and we exchanged kisses.

"Good-night, Niko," he said to me emotionally and turned quickly to leave.

"Good-night, Peter."

The name Peter came spontaneously to my lips, without my intending to call him that. But he was taken aback, as though I had hit him from behind.

He turned around and stared at me.

"Not you, too?" he said, simply.

1984

It all happened in the village of Vlychos, on the island of Lesbos, in the summer of 1962. Marika, wife of Demosthenes Keramaris, had been planning for some years to have a small chapel built as a memorial and final resting place for her parents, Nikolaos and Arete Kokkinos. Her husband had been looking for an excuse not to become involved. But the couple were childless, a fact that seemed not completely unrelated to the offering under consideration. Marika persisted and finally, in the face of her tenacity, Demosthenes Keramaris decided to begin construction of the chapel.

The southeast corner of the family olive grove, located in Lygies, on the outskirts of the village, was chosen as the most suitable site. The olive grove—part of Marika's dowry—was adjacent to the old, stone-paved road that led to the sea; at a distance of not more than three minutes from there was a hand-hewn Turkish fountain.

Work on the project began on April 23 of the same year. In the process of digging out the ground for the foundation, at a depth of about one meter, the workers hit upon some ancient ruins with their pickaxes. Soon two capitals were unearthed, then some fragments of a vase, and a skeleton from whose skull the lower jawbone was missing. On the roof of the palate a piece of tile was found with three Byzantine crosses roughly carved on it. At the insistence of the contractor, who had experience in such matters—and with the addition of another worker to the crew—the work continued; the foundation was quickly laid, and the building was completed in nine days. The bones that had been dug up were put in an old woolen sack and left lying beneath an olive tree. When the foreman, Michael Vrontamas, attempted, for some reason, to move the sack, he discovered that it was impossible, but, shortly afterward, he claimed to have done this quite easily after crossing himself in terror beforehand. The workman Leonidas Frantzis said that precisely one day earlier, as he was bending down to pick up a certain tool from under the olive tree, he tripped over the sack, from within which he heard a noise and a deep groan.

The bones, shut in a perfectly proportioned cedar chest, were deposited at the holy site of the newly built chapel. A woman named Magdalene Drakopoulou insists that the bones are still moving and groaning. She states that she heard them herself, and that their movements and groans ceased as soon as she gave them a few drops of water.

The occasion of the unearthing of the skeleton was the cause for much discussion. Some of the older people remembered that in the ruins upon which the chapel had been erected there had once been a monastery; for years, a monk used to appear there; the place was considered haunted. Tradition has it that the Turks had slaughtered some Christian monks in that very spot.

Chrysanthe Frantzis, wife of the above-mentioned workman, recounted that as she was carrying food to her husband, while the chapel was still being built, she saw an emaciated, robe-clad stranger inside and fled in a state of panic. That night she saw the Virgin Mary in a dream. "You need not have been afraid," she said to her. "The man you saw was the monk who used to live here. He is a saint. One day you will learn his name and his entire story."

Several weeks later the following occurred: Paraskevi Aiserkiti, an eighty-six-year-old woman, had been on her deathbed for three days and three nights, because her younger daughter-in-law—the wife of her youngest son—horrified by the family tradition, had refused to squeeze her neck so that she could exhale her dying breath. On the fourth night of her ordeal she thought that God had taken pity on her. But the man standing before her was not her guardian angel. "I am a saint," he said to her. "Have faith in me and come kneel down before my bones. I will make you well."

Paraskevi Aiserkiti wanted to shout out to him that she was a sinner but her voice would not come out. Helpless, she could do nothing but cry, and her tears came down like a river, only to be lost in yet another river of perspiration running down from her brow. "You must wash your heel in that spot," commanded the saint, as layer upon layer of sin peeled off her body.

The next morning she regained her senses for a short while. She was able to speak and she recounted her dream to her children. They took her to the small chapel. She fell on her knees and kissed the bones now being kept for posterity in that holy place, and she immediately became well.

Several days later the monk appeared to Marika Keramaris in her sleep. "I am the venerable Saint Rafael," he said to her. "The bones you found belong to me. The Turks tortured us cruelly and then butchered us with a hacksaw. I am a saint and I shall perform many miracles."

Marika Keramaris bowed her head, ready to ask him to grant her what she had been denied by life: a child. She was prevented from doing so by the thought that perhaps, for a woman her age, this might seem indecent to the saint, and she snuffed out the desire smoldering within her. She told her dream to no one but her husband. Both were astonished when they learned that their fellow villager, Konstantine Vrachnos, as he was preparing for bed one night, had heard a voice calling out to him: "My name is Rafael."

That night the saint was also seen by the night watchman of the neighboring village of Moires. The saint said to the watchman, "I come from Ithaca," and he asked that an icon of himself be made.

Four days later he once again appeared to Marika Keramaris in her sleep. He wore the robes of a canon. "I have come to finish my story," he said to her. "I came to Lesbos after the fall of Constantinople, in 1454, when the Turks invaded Thrace. Go and convey this to the bishop."

The very same night the saint appeared to a fourteen-year-old schoolboy, Alfeios Matzouranis. He said to him, "I am not alone. Near the chapel is the grave of my deacon, Nikolaos. You will find his bones. Be most careful, for he, too, is a saint."

Subsequently, the venerable Rafael appeared to the following women: Virginia Manoussi, Mirsini Dorkofiki, Vassiliki Komporosou, Maria Tsaliki, Mirsini Marangou, Angeliki Marangou, and Adamantia Lykiardopoulou. Each one asked him where the grave of Nikolaos was. He indicated the location by making the sign of the cross. When, the following day, Demosthenes Keramaris went out with his workmen to dig, the above-mentioned women had planted a short rod in the very same spot, at the site of which the ground was elevated into a small, earthy mound.

The excavation was soon under way, and Nikolaos's skeleton was uncovered at about the same depth, one meter down. His head was facing west and his feet were pointing east. Beside him lay a pectoral cross made out of silver and lead, with icons of the Mother of Our Lord and of the Archangel carved in relief on either side. One of the women lifted the almost-calcified skull, brushed the dirt from it, and washed it with wine. Then, from behind the faulty ridge of its teeth, a fragment of tile was dislodged, with three Byzantine crosses on it, also hand-carved. A short distance from the grave were two earthenware jugs with broken spouts. Inside them were the remains of some charred bones, a child's mummified hand, and the venerable Rafael's lower jawbone, which had not been found among the rest of his bones. The workmen performing the excavation, Ioannis Bakourouglou and Sofianos Portaras, were the first to discover the pectoral cross, which was given over to the custody of the island's curator of antiquities. At the exact moment when the earth was parted and the skeletal remains came into view, it began to drizzle, and in this way a prophesy made by the archdeacon Nikolaos to Mirsini Marangou in a dream was fulfilled, for he had said to her: "You will find my bones under rain."

The removal of the relics was completed in late afternoon, on July 16, on the eve of the Feast of Saint Marina. Demosthenes Keramaris paid the workmen, returned to his home, slaughtered a rooster for the following day's meal, bathed, and went for a stroll in the village marketplace as twilight began to fall. While he was out, his wife boiled some water in order to remove the down from the slain rooster, and as she was dipping it into the boiling water she remembered that it was their wedding anniversary that day. They had been married for eighteen years. They were already middle-aged. She was forty-three and her husband fifty-four.

That night, in bed, Demosthenes Keramaris reached out his hand to caress her, but for several reasons, only one being that it was a holiday eve, she did not respond. Demosthenes Keramaris soon fell off to sleep and did not persist.

1988

The party was being held outdoors and the participants were men, exclusively. We were losing Markos Monachos. He was getting married in a few days and we, his friends, gathered there to mourn him— that kind of party.

I ran to the bank of the stream for a moment to urinate and saw Takis S. on the other side coming toward me with a smile. Pink of cheek, clean-shaven, with a clean shirt and tie on and not a trace of dirt on him, in spite of the fact that he had died recently. He came up close to me, gave me a hug, and kissed me on the mouth. I had no time to gag, or get scared. Then, from the same direction came— what was his name, again? I couldn't remember. He came up next to me. Another kiss. He, too, was dead. I still couldn't remember who he was. Sick to my stomach, with the taste of death still on my lips, I thought I simply had to tell my dream to someone, so that it wouldn't come true. That very instant I recounted it to my buddies at the party. One of them said, "It's the Nether Ones."

I carried that taste around in my mouth for two days. On the third I borrowed a small truck to haul sea sand. The chief constructor needed sea sand. I went down to Skopas Tegea and loaded twenty sacks. I had the sun behind me. "What a light," I kept repeating, "what a light." It was the end of October.

I felt drowsy. "I will stop at the inn," I said to myself, "order coffee, and wash my face." There were about six hundred meters still ahead of me, which I never did cover. When I started falling, I tried to keep my eyes open but it was impossible. "The Nether Ones," I kept thinking, and waited to be killed. The truck plunged downward, engine first. It struck something, turned over, crashed again, turned a second time, and then a third. Though I was inside, I could still follow the curves—gruesome and perfectly symmetrical—traced by the fall. With the fourth crash it struck something and began to shake, eventually wedging itself in the narrow bed of the ravine, its wheels mocking heaven. I had not been killed, and in the unbearable stillness that followed I was expecting to hear the explosion from the first jet of a large flame that had sprung up, but that didn't happen either. I then began kicking the windowpane of the door with my right foot, trying to break it. I was wearing rubber-soled boots, and the glass was also rubbery and resistant and wouldn't break.

I will not go into the panic I felt at that moment.

1991

To Stelios K.

ROSES FOR MARIA A.

I   They were yelling and swearing at each other. At a certain point Skarpathiotakis grabbed a knife, but we stopped him. Vouros went back to his table and continued drinking beers with the others. Skarpathiotakis remained alone, drinking orange juice. A little later he went over to Vouros and asked him what time it was. Then he said: "In twenty minutes you're going to die." And he walked out.

     He came back almost immediately. He came into the club very quickly, holding a gun. Three shots rang out. We ran and grabbed Skarpathiotakis, but he managed to fire three more shots. Vouros stood up, clutching his face, but then he fell to the floor. And Skarpathiotakis left. He turned and left with his gun in his hand. Then someone said that they had been fighting over a woman.

II   They had arranged to meet at Kastella, at the bus stop on that wide bend in the road. The girls had gotten dressed up for the evening. At ten after seven Michalis arrived.

     "Let's get going," he said.

     "What about Tolis?"

     "He's coming with Kosmas. They'll meet us in the square."

     A trolley came along and they got on it. It wasn't quite dark yet. In the harbor of Faliron, the Sixth Fleet was anchored. When they reached the square they sat down at the Edelweiss. They found a table in the back from which they could see the passersby outside through the windows.

     At nine-thirty Tolis arrived with Kosmas.

     "You're late," Michalis said.

Tolis's hair was still very short, but he wasn't wearing his navy uniform.

Kosmas looked at the girls proudly.

"He's AWOL," he said, slapping Tolis on the back.

They pulled up chairs and sat down with the rest of the group.

"Drinks are on me," said Tolis, offering them some whiskey.

"We're hungry," said the girls.

Kosmas suggested a new pizza place in Piraïkí.

"No," said Michalis. "Not pizza."

"How about shrimp?" said the first Maria.

Tolis stood up on the double.

"Shrimp it is," he repeated.

They went outside and hailed a taxi. There were six of them.

"Maria will sit on my lap," said Michalis, smiling to himself.

Which Maria did he mean? Either he hadn't realized that they had the hots for each other or he was just trying to provoke Tolis.

They crowded into the taxi. There was no time for the close bodily contact to excite them. The restaurant was in Nikaia, on the corner of General Kalaris Street and Oudemision Street. It was so big it looked almost like a football stadium, and they only served seafood. Mostly shrimp: boiled shrimp, fried shrimp, grilled shrimp, shrimp flambé.

They ordered scallops and a chilled, white wine. The shrimp came next. The girls began eating with knives and forks but quickly stopped.

"Use your fingers," said Kosmas, breaking their tender armor with ease and sucking knowingly on the shells.

Vicky laughed, titillated, and was the first to follow his example. Her painted nails had a wet sheen to them, and they glimmered beneath the neon lights on the roof.

They ordered more wine. And then more. The waiters hurried back and forth, trying to catch their breath, through the noisy crowd. Next they ordered fruit. The other Maria picked up a piece of apple with her fingers and put it in Michalis's glass. It was an encouraging gesture. He put another piece in her glass.

"Tonight I'm not getting drunk," said Michalis. "Not tonight."
And he emptied his glass, bottoms up.

A boy came over with flowers. Tolis bought all the roses he had
on him and threw them at the first Maria's feet.

"He must be celebrating something," said Vicky, looking at Tolis
and feigning surprise.

"It's a secret," said Kosmas.

The first Maria smiled demurely and gave Vicky a rose. Then she
gave one to the other Maria.

Then they got up to leave.

"I'm paying," said Tolis.

Michalis cut him short.

"No way."

"Let them work it out for themselves," said the first Maria, as she
made for the exit.

She walked on ahead, sure of herself and satisfied. The other
two girls followed her. They went outside and waited for the men,
shifting their weight from side to side as they stood there in their
high-heeled shoes. The alcohol had already begun to take effect on
them, and they could feel it, in their moist underarms, slowly and
pleasantly overpowering them.

A taxi appeared up the road, and Michalis, who had just come
through the door at that moment, raised his hand and hailed it. There
were still six of them, and the taxi driver said they wouldn't all fit.
A second taxi came and pulled up alongside them.

"We'll take this one," said Kosmas, and pulled Vicky inside with him.

"See you at Mon Amour," Michalis shouted to him, as they pulled
quickly away.

The boulevard was deserted, and the two taxis sped along, one
behind the other. They reached the "river" and turned right just
before the bridge. For a while they went slowly along the riverbank,
following the cracked asphalt paving. Then they stopped at a big,

empty lot. The two Marias got out first, followed by Michalis and
Tolis. Vicky and Kosmas joined them. A row of sparsely hung light-
bulbs lit up the parking lot, and they could hear the muted, muffled
sounds of music coming from the darkened nightclub across the way.

"Let's get out of here," the first Maria said suddenly.

For some inexplicable reason she seemed to be feeling uneasy.
Tolis took her by the hand.

"Let's go and dance," he said, practically dragging her along
after him.

They went past the porter, who tipped his cap and bowed
courteously.

It was one-fifteen when they went inside. Their ears were immediately assaulted by the intensity of the wild, provocative sounds coming from the loudspeakers. They asked for a table near the dance floor
but they had to wait. There were no tables available. Michalis saw
someone waving to him from the other end of the room. He went over
to him and said hello. It was a fellow he knew from Kallithea. They
used to work out together at the Piraïkós gym, in the amateur section,
doing Greco-Roman wrestling. While they were standing there talking, the first Maria tossed all her roses to the group of people sitting
next to her, climbed up on their table, and began doing a belly dance.
No one expected her to do something like that. Her body had been
taken over by the music. A man of about fifty, his shirt open all the way
down to his navel, kneeled down in front of her and began clapping his
hands. Then he ordered some plates to throw and to break.

"What a whore," said Tolis.

He was furious but he controlled himself. Kosmas went over to
Papakongos and asked him to sing a couple of songs.

"Which songs do you want?" asked Tolis.

Then they saw the girls leaving the room. Kosmas ran after
them. The first Maria went into the ladies room. The other two stood
waiting a few steps further on.

"What's going on?" asked Kosmas.

They didn't have time to answer. The girl selling balloons ran out into the hall, terror-stricken, shouting to someone. A tall, stocky man ran over to her. There were suddenly a lot of people jammed inside the doorway, as two men holding Tolis under his arms pushed him firmly out the door. They left him next to the coat-check room. The music was still blaring with the same intensity. The tall man went over and stood in front of him.

"Take it easy," he said, in a quiet, almost friendly tone of voice.

Tolis's jacket was ruffled around the collar and two buttons were missing from it. Tolis tugged at it, trying to straighten it, then felt discreetly under his belt.

"Everything's fine," he said.

He saw the first Maria coming out of the ladies room. Her lips were bright red, like a knife slash. He quietly but swiftly darted past the two men barring the door and went back into the dance hall. Kosmas ran in behind him. The tall man tried to block his way, and Kosmas charged at him, head first, ramming into his stomach.

He found an empty bottle somewhere and held it by the neck. He didn't really know who he was trying to scare. Then the music stopped. He heard Tolis screaming. It was the battle cry of the attacker. He's taking his "revenge," thought Kosmas. Just then some men jumped on him and threw him down, pieces of broken glass cutting into his hands. They dragged him away and locked him in the kitchen.

There was a window open. Kosmas pulled himself up with difficulty, climbed through it, and found himself in the backyard. He heard the sound of high-heeled shoes and all at once saw the three girls running toward the parking lot. He called them and they came over to him. Vicky was trembling, in a panic.

"Tolis left," said the second Maria.

"Alone?"

"Yes."

They climbed over a dark, dilapidated fence and came out on the main road.

The empty lot in front of the nightclub looked deserted and quiet, as though nothing had happened. They began walking quickly away. It was cool and a faint breeze was blowing. Kosmas looked behind him once or twice, without slowing his pace. Soon the sun would be rising. They stopped the first taxi that came along and got in.

"Leonidion Street," said Kosmas.

Tolis was already there. He had washed his hands and his face, but his shirt had blood on it. He took a dark sweatshirt and put it on over his shirt.

"You'd better change, too," he said to Kosmas. Then he asked what had happened to Michalis.

"I don't know," said Kosmas.

The girls started crying.

"That's enough," said Tolis. "You stay here."

He packed a small bag with his navy uniform and a change of clothing.

"Let's go," he said to Kosmas.

They went out into the street. The sun was almost up and they walked in silence to the next corner.

"Do you like the first Maria?" Kosmas asked Tolis.

"As a woman, yes. But I don't like her much as a person. And when she's with me I want her to behave like a lady."

They came to the bus stop near the bridge. Across from them was the old thread mill with the ceramic goddesses at each end of its tiled roof.

"Don't go to work, because if they catch you they'll accuse you of being an accomplice at the scene of the crime."

Kosmas said nothing, and Tolis left him at the bus stop and went off.

He went to Tabouria, to Maratheas's house. They had worked together once in the harbor, in the reserves. And they had gotten their first deferments together, from the battleship *Palaska*. He knocked on the door; it was almost six in the morning. He knocked and Maratheas himself appeared. He was in his underwear.

"How'd you like some company?"

"Come on in," said Maratheas.

He left him in the hall and went to get dressed. He came back shortly afterward.

"What are you doing here so early?"

"There was some trouble at Mon Amour. I'm looking for a hideout for forty-eight hours."

Maratheas's wife appeared in the hall, wearing a long bathrobe. She went into the bathroom, brushed her hair, and came back out.

Maratheas got up to go.

"I won't be long," he said.

He left and his wife stayed. She was tall and full-bodied. They called her Queenie.

"Queenie, I'm thirsty," Tolis said to her.

He had his knife in its sheath and the sheath attached to his waist.

She brought him a stiff drink of rakí and half an eggplant, stuffed.

"After what you've done, you'll wind up in prison in Aigina," she said to him.

Tolis left the glass on the table without touching it.

"Queenie, if I have to worry about your calling the police every time I go to the bathroom, it's better if I leave."

After about an hour Maratheas came back.

"I found somebody who'll hide you," he said.

"Can he be trusted?"

"Yes."

"Who is he?"

It was Thomás Diamantopoulos. He was Maratheas's brother-in-law and he was a bachelor. Maratheas gave him the address, and Tolis went and found him there. He lived in Moschaton, in an old one-story house. Diamantopoulos showed him a room that looked out on the backyard.

"You'll stay here."

The yard was covered by a large, climbing vine. There was mint and lavender growing along the surrounding wall.

"While I'm away I don't want you to be heard or seen," said Diamantopoulos. "This is a good neighborhood." And he left.

He came back at lunchtime with a roasted chicken.

"Are you hungry?" he asked Tolis, and he went into the kitchen and set the table. Then the telephone rang.

Diamantopoulos went into the living room, closing the sliding glass doors behind him.

"Hello," he said.

Tolis tried to listen in, but Diamantopoulos did not talk. He only listened. Finally he said "all right" and hung up the phone. He went back into the kitchen and continued cutting the chicken.

Tolis looked at him, still standing.

"Sit down," Diamantopoulos said to him.

Then he asked him, "Dark meat or white?"

"Dark," said Tolis.

They began eating in silence.

"I have mustard," said Diamantopoulos, and he got up and went to the refrigerator.

He took out a plastic jar shaped like a piglet.

"Who was it?" asked Tolis.

Diamantopoulos looked at him.

"On the phone."

"Maratheas."

"What did he say?"

"That you did a lot of damage. You wasted two guys and one of them was a cop out of uniform. They had the joint cased for angel dust. Dedoussis is after your head."

"Did he tell you to get rid of me?"

Diamantopoulos didn't answer. He put some mustard on his plate and then he pushed it over to Tolis.

"I have a friend who deals in illegal spices," he said.

Tolis listened to him without speaking.

"He could help you escape, if you want," said Diamantopoulos.

"Escape where?"

"Abroad."

His answer stunned Tolis. It was logical and had been thought out in advance.

"For how much?" he asked after a while.

"I have to speak with him first," said Diamantopoulos. And he began the bargaining by saying, "Maybe two hundred thousand would be enough."

Tolis had no luck. He had played the football lottery and had guessed the scores of eleven games. Eleven out of seven hundred and twenty-eight. Ninety-four thousand three hundred and sixty drachmas. It was enough to buy drinks at the nightclub and to buy those roses for the first Maria. If only he hadn't listened to Gerasimos. He had insisted that he bet on all the sure wins. If he had only trusted his instinct. If he had just followed his hunch not to bet on those two favorites, he would have been the only one to get thirteen games right.

"I can find eighty thousand," said Tolis. "And I'm willing to part with it to save my neck."

"I have to discuss it with my friend first."

His friend was Dedoussis, the policeman. Diamantopoulos had already spoken to him. Tolis saw him gaze shiftily from side to side. He got up.

"Okay," he said. "Don't bother. You don't have to have me around anymore. You haven't seen me and you don't know where I am."

He took his jacket and went out into the tiny garden.

"So long," he said to Diamantopoulos.

He started turning into a street on his right.

"Not right, go to the left," shouted Diamantopoulos.

Tolis turned left and at the next corner saw Officer Dedoussis in front of him with about ten more men. He was holding handcuffs and the others had guns.

"Give yourself up, Tolis," said the policeman.

Then he turned to his men.

"Get him," he said.

Two men stepped forward and moved toward him.

Tolis threw his jacket at them and drew his knife.

"Aim for his legs," said the policeman.

Someone came up behind him and was about to hit him with an iron bar. Tolis ducked suddenly and turned on his heels until he was facing him, pointing his knife straight ahead.

"His legs," he heard the policeman say again.

And suddenly his knees buckled under. They wanted to arrest him, not kill him. He pulled slightly away and realized that they had broken his left shinbone. "Bastards," he muttered between his teeth. He stopped, out of breath, and looked at the policemen, who were still hesitant to approach him. A wave of anger swept over him. He'd gotten away with two deferments and two indictments for insubordination, and here he was in the hands of the police. It was all over now. He raised his knife high, in a rage. He wanted to plunge it into his stomach but before he could lift it up high enough, he was jolted by a strong blow. He let go of his knife as the pain reached his heart. His wrist felt like it had been torn to shreds. "They turned me in," he thought. Maratheas and Diamantopoulos. And then he passed out.

"Do you like the first Maria?" he heard himself asking, his face in the dirt.

1991

The landscape was not quite a landscape. It was a photograph. But it was no ordinary photograph. It was, rather, a small sea promontory. I could recognize the place, but when did I get there? I was unable to remember and this upset me. Using a magnifying lens, I began checking the tops of the rocks. I tried examining, painstakingly, the narrow crevasses that rose up by degrees, eroded by the sea water, as my agitation increased. I then changed my mind. Instead of searching through the lens I turned the sheet of paper over: It was as obvious as it was easy. Right there on the reverse side was the real landscape. At the tip of the cape shone the white light of Chrysopege, the Church of the Golden Source. It was twenty years earlier, yet somehow not in the past.

I stopped by the small chapel and looked around. There was nothing in the air. As I turned to leave, in disappointment, I heard Poppy calling me. She looked just as she did then. She moved toward me.

"Isn't this what you wanted? To come back to these rocks?"

The memories the sound of her voice brought back! Back then, we had made love on those rocks. Something stirred deep inside me. That was it. That was why I was so agitated. I could see it at last. That was what I wanted. But we couldn't attempt it just then.

"Why not?" Poppy asked.

"We need to get out of this place."

"Out of this place?" She looked at me with surprise.

There was a cement bell tower behind the church. I was seeing it for the first time. Not exactly a bell tower, it was a water tower minus the tank at the top. This upset me considerably, but I felt I had to go on.

"We are twenty years behind," I told her. "We can't do anything. Reality does not repeat itself. We need to get out of here."

She seemed not to understand.

"We need to go forward," I said to her.

"Back into the photograph?"

"Yes, there is no other way."

She smiled condescendingly.

"It's impossible to go through. The cape cannot turn over. It's not made of paper."

A feeling of wild desperation swept over me. I took her by the hand. "Come," I said. "We will go through."

And we did, at last. We went through the pores of the coarse-grained photograph, which were also pores and grains of salt.

We lay down in the same crag, just like the first time, and Poppy spread a sheet over us. She's become modest, I thought. She wanted to undress and she did not want me to see her.

"I've had two daughters and I've lost my figure," she said.

"Don't blame me. Your daughters aren't mine."

"That's what I blame you for most."

She was angry and hurt; or did she want to hurt me?

Suddenly she threw the sheet off, got up and, stepping from one crack to the next, began climbing down. This time she did not mind my seeing her naked. She stopped at the edge of the sea and, bending down, dipped her hands in the water. She was no longer the wild prairie, I could appreciate that. Her figure had not changed much, she had simply become arable. My love could now spread itself comfortably on the high plateaus of her waist. My poor, starved love.

She got up and turned my way, holding something that resembled a sea urchin. It was not, in fact, a sea urchin; it was a sea porcupine.

"It's the Day of the Transfiguration," she called to me. She was absolutely radiant in her maturity.

"The Transfiguration of our Lord and Savior," I said. "On this day August 6, 1991."

1991

DEEP BLUE ALMOST BLACK

A NOVELLA

To *Sigi H.*
17.VI.77

All I know is that one day I woke up not feeling quite right. I just couldn't stay put in my bed, but that used to happen to me sometimes. Then it started to happen regularly, it was like I couldn't get away from my own self. At first I thought I could escape from myself by spending time with other people. Then even that began to bore me. What could other people tell me that I didn't already know? They say that work can help you forget yourself, but it's a lie, it's like being on pills. As soon as their effect wears off, you have to start all over again. You'd have to work twenty-four hours a day or something, but who can stand that? I do write things down here and there. I've told you about that. Right now I haven't written a thing because I've been running around all day. How could I have given away my dog? That dog of mine who only ate chocolate, how could I? That was the end. And then there was my poet, but since I couldn't just give him away, I decided to give him my couch from Skyros and move back to my parents' house. It was such a relief and yet I did so much crying. But then it's always been difficult for me to break up with people I want to leave. My God, it's always so much trouble. I was married to that poet for twenty-two months. Just two months short of two years. He was terribly fussy about the way he dressed, especially about matching colors—socks, sweater, and all the rest. That was his armor for the long march to eternity, as he himself liked to put it. I don't think he was joking. He was a confirmed narcissist, and he meant it.

Days, and nights, so beautiful.

Everything's always so beautiful with me. I can't read any more of this stuff. It's all so hard to read. You see what's going on here. I have to start pulling myself together a little. I think I should shut myself up at home and start putting some order in my mind.

Well, that's it. Anyway, I've moved into a new mode now. Really. Now I'm a woman in a hurry, I'm no longer a dreamer. My Uncle Carolos, when he was seventy-two, used to flush the toilet even before peeing. Isn't that a form of panic? Of course he died at the age of ninety—almost. Don't laugh. And my Uncle Costas, he's going on eighty now. Mama still calls him a kid. He lost his wife two years ago. Beautiful, blond Despina. Blond in her youth, I mean. She died of a heart attack. She was short and full of energy and much younger than he was, about sixty, that is. It was only two years ago and already he goes out every single day. Off he goes to his office, as handsome as can be, every single day. His skin has such a healthy-looking shine to it, it makes you feel like kissing him. He hurries along from the square where he lives down to the corner of Stadiou and Omirou. All the way downtown, with his arms clasped behind him, almost running. Every single day, in such a rush, always hurrying to be on time, but for what? And in the evening he usually invites two or three ladies, widows of friends, out to dinner and they go to different restaurants. Eighty years old. That's why I believe I'll die old. All the Moudros die old. That's terrible. I don't want to die old. I really don't, but I can't keep telling you the same things over and over again. I'm not in good shape. Maybe because yesterday I talked too much again. I seem to have to be a little drunk so I can talk. I feel more at ease that way. Otherwise I don't open my mouth. But I can't constantly be a little drunk because I'll end up an alcoholic. I have nothing else to say. My life is no longer of interest. Even so, I sometimes get incredibly angry with myself. It's anger at remembering. All those traps you get yourself caught in, through your own doing. Beautiful eyes, beautiful words, and all that. There are people who

help you to deceive yourself. Only you always realize it too late.
Remembering is so unpleasant for me. But here I go again, you see.
Times were different in Paris. I had to work so I could earn money.
We didn't have enough, as usual. I was always drawn to people who
were broke. Strange, isn't it, although two of my husbands had quite
a lot of money. I worked in a boutique. I don't know why I ever took
that job. I guess I was going through a difficult time. Or maybe I just
wanted to think I was. Anyway, I had to work. All kinds of ladies
would come in to shop for clothes, and because I was used to doing
whatever I pleased all my life, I would get insulted. It was awful, they
were all so rude. I would stand there thinking that even in their
wildest dreams they couldn't imagine what it was like to be brought
up the way I had been. Then I would start getting really mad because
they were being so ridiculous. I used to feel like throwing their pack-
ages right in their faces. I just wasn't cut out for that kind of work. It
didn't suit me at all. But none of this is of very much interest when
I'm not in good spirits. Only if I have a little drink, then I can face it
all with a certain sense of humor. But I shouldn't because at five-
thirty Nicole and I are supposed to go down to the airport. We'll be
picking up some Dutchman. Nicole is in public relations. She kind of
stole the job away from me. From accounting to public relations. I
can't understand how all my life I've never saved any money. It bothers me that I won't be able to do whatever I feel like anymore. All my
life I've been spending so much money. I never thought that someday
I might need it. Or maybe it's because I've never found myself in a
position of real need. I always spent whatever I had. There are some
very stingy people around, including some who are quite close to
me. That's a terrible fault, really. I think people used to be more gen-
erous before. They would send you presents, and show you that they
cared about you. Now nobody cares, and especially if you're not
young anymore. In the end all that matters is your physical appearance. Because if you have smooth skin and bright eyes and all those

things, then you've really got it made. That's the way it is. But people
are so vain, and especially my present husband. He likes beautiful
women, beautiful cars. He once had a prewar Citroën, and he used to
drive it all around Kolonaki. One of those cars with a running board
and large wings. Of course, I used to think the same way myself when
I was young. I thought that being beautiful was everything. Now I
don't care anymore. I could live with an ugly person, as long as he
was clever and kind. I made a mistake, I shouldn't have married a
man like my husband. I get the feeling that I'm living with someone
who's only staying with me because we happen to be married. I
should probably get a divorce, but then I'd be all alone. And the problem is that tomorrow the same thing will start all over again. I read an
article about that on Sunday. In the end neither the woman who has
managed to liberate herself through working nor the woman who is a
wife, mother, or whatever, is happy. Nobody is happy. I don't think
it's any fun to be alone. But you can end up alone by becoming a
widow, too. I don't know. It would be nice if you could have a husband who was away somewhere and you could wait for him and think
about his coming back. The real problem is whether or not you can
live with the truth. I'm so upset, Nicole used to say: I can't understand it, Michalis is coming back. He's coming tomorrow and here I
am all upset. And then I'd tell her: It's because for a whole year you
were free to go wherever you wanted, and now with Michalis around
you'll be going everywhere as a twosome, like a pair of dummies.
That must be it, she would say. She would think for a while and then
she would say: Well, I just don't see what can be done about your
problem. What can we do about it? She meant about me being such a
wreck. She used to see me like that so often, it was awful. You have to
get yourself a boyfriend, she would say: Get out and have a good
time. All the while laughing like crazy. Go hang out. Out where? It's
like telling you to let your breasts hang out. It's ridiculous. She would
tell me: Nine out of ten women have boyfriends, even at our age.

Then I would say: And what's the point of that? And we'd go on and
on like that. Nicole, strutting along in those spike-heeled shoes of
hers. She's a Sagittarius. They say that's the sign of polygamy. I'm a
Capricorn and a very pessimistic one at that. Leo is also a very tire-
some star sign. I've had three of them in my life. And all three of
them gave me an incredibly hard time. Two men and one woman.
Perversions, perversions. I was sure that's what you'd say. No, I never
had any leanings toward women. She was just a friend. I liked her but
she was sneaky, always chasing after men. They say that Capricorns
have a slow, complex pattern of development. I really wish I were a
Sagittarius. I actually know someone who can tell immediately what
sign a person is, and he never makes a mistake. It's been his hobby
since he was very young, and he spends all his time studying the
signs. Once there were forty of us, and he would try and guess what
sign someone was. Then he would ask them and he'd be right. One
person after another, he'd get them all right. All of them. Strange. Of
course I don't believe in any of that, all that nonsense they write in
magazines. Today this will happen to you. You'll meet so and so, some
money will come to you. But maybe there's some truth in it. Our
health, for example. They say that Leos suffer from heart trouble,
Capricorns are prone to sensitive stomachs, and so on. Maybe some
overall patterns do exist, some similarities. I don't know. There are
differences, too, of course. Leo, so crazy and unpredictable. When he
came back last summer my husband started looking through one
magazine after another to find out what was going to happen to him.
All those awful magazines. Like a maniac. And he was the one who
never paid any attention to the future, never took the slightest notice
of it. Maybe it was because of the bad company he'd been keeping.
Maybe it was because he'd taken up with some silly woman who read
her horoscope every day. When we had our first big quarrel, I said to
my sister-in-law: Our first big fight. I told her: Your brother is the
only person I've ever met who has no dreams. He's never said "we

will." We'll do this, we'll do that, we'll do anything, in fact. The only time he ever said "we will" was before we got married. He said he would take me to Agrapha. That was fifteen years ago. He promised me that one day he would take me to Agrapha as his wife. It was very nice to hear. He never took me there. I guess he saw me as the bride one takes to his village. How is it possible to live with a person and not to know him? I know, of course, that he was in love with someone, and that when she was dying he went to her and stayed there until she died and watched her take her last breath. But when all is said and done, what difference does any of this make? And I'm so tired right now that I'm afraid I'll have to drag myself through the evening again and that I'll be bored with the Dutchman. I won't open my mouth and the dinner will turn out all wrong because I'll be feeling tired. We'll go to L'Abreuvoir, up near Dexameni Square. Not near Dexameni, near that other place, the old Omorpho. I don't see why I should even bother going since it doesn't seem like fun. Actually, I often decide to go anyway and then I have a good time, through my own efforts, because I entertain myself. I talk a lot and I laugh at what I'm saying, and in the end the evening turns out okay. Not that every single evening has to turn out perfect, of course. But why bother about all this, evenings that turn out okay or evenings that don't. I don't know. Maybe it's just because I'm tired. Because I didn't sleep well last night. Or because of a whole lot of other things. Maybe if you made me a coffee I would feel better. For a long time now I just fall apart when I haven't had any sleep. You, of course, wouldn't even think of coming to my house. I guess you're put off by the doorman. I was scared of him, too, in the beginning, until I discovered that it was his eyes. There's something wrong with his eyes, they don't focus together, but you don't realize it at first and you feel like he has something against you. Like he's holding some secret grudge against you. Silly little things like that can ruin your whole day. Especially when you have worries of your own.

I went out this morning to go to the bank and I saw a cat there
on the corner. I don't think it was hurt, there was no blood on it anywhere, but it was dying. I thought of getting someone to come and
give it an injection, like they do in northern Europe. In England they
give them a quick injection and put them out of their misery. It was
awful, that process of dying going on and on. Then I went to the bank
and I came back, because of course I had the cat on my mind the
whole time. It had really got to me. It was strange. It was dying, and it
had opened its mouth and kept putting its paws in front of its eyes.
Some children had gathered round and were shouting: its eyes are
open, its eyes are open. I told them to leave it alone, not to bother
the cat. Because they just couldn't understand that it wasn't doing
that because it felt like it. Luckily it died after that. I left, and until
the afternoon that scene continued to bother me. I wanted to pick it
up in my arms right then and there and comfort it, but it was impossible, I didn't have the courage. I was in such a bad state of mind that I
couldn't even pick it up. I would have collapsed in the middle of the
street and made a fool of myself. I would have started crying over the
cat and the whole street would have stopped and they'd start saying I
was crazy. And then, the way people are in my neighborhood, how
could I explain to them that I am a bit crazy. That's not just being
oversensitive, that's neurotic. We live in such an ocean of memories,
photographs, etcetera, etcetera, that if any of it is disturbed, it's bad.
Maybe it's because of the age we're at. Many years ago my father and I
were driving to Sounion and we ran into a jeep. It was a long time
ago. The jeep turned over and everyone in it ended up underneath it.
There were three young couples, and I ran to see what had happened
to all those people. I wasn't the least bit afraid. I was just trying to
prevent my father from coming too near because he had a heart condition and I wanted to keep him away. Fortunately they were all fine.
They had gotten to their feet and were struggling to turn the jeep
back onto its wheels. They hadn't been seriously hurt and they were

having a great time, as a matter of fact. When you're young you can allow yourself to do all kinds of things. The bad thing is that I feel very, very young, but other people don't see me that way. You're acting like a small child, they tell me. Well, what's so bad about being a small child? They say it as if it were wrong that I never grew up. Why should that be wrong? I can't understand it. Perhaps I'm immature. I don't know. Anyway, it's an advantage that's of no use to anyone, and certainly not to me. But I don't even know that for sure. In the end it doesn't really matter. I don't know what I am, I don't know what I'm doing. Perhaps I do know what I'm thinking. But then again, it's as if you don't have the right to think what you want, as if even that is wrong. Maybe I need a doctor. It seems I have some kind of block, that certain mechanisms aren't quite functioning properly. I read that psychotherapy is most effective before the age of forty-five. That you can have amazing results before you're forty-five. But I'm past the age limit. Of course, if a person is clever and if she really wants to, there is no limit. By limit I don't mean that someone has to be a hundred years old. What can you change in a hundred-year-old? "Daddy, how long do turtles live?" "Two or three hundred years." "And then what, Daddy?" "Then, fiddlesticks." Before the age of forty-five. Nonsense. I don't believe it's possible to build a new person out of someone who's fallen completely apart. You mustn't tamper with such things. It must be difficult to put someone back together without throwing his inner world into turmoil. I wonder if there are any people who are well. It seems to me that we're all a bit sick, more or less. But what's sick and what isn't? What's good and what's bad? Good is what's good for us and bad is what's bad for us. Good and Bad don't exist. High-minded philosophizing. It's because I question a whole lot of things, all the time. I believe them and I don't believe them. Half of my mind says yes, the other half no. So then it doesn't really matter since my mind is always equally divided. I survive with half my mind here and half over there. Anyway, there must be some-

thing, a mold or a cast of some kind. No, not a cast, but maybe a set
of restraints of some kind that keep people in check. An inhibitive
force that restores our equilibrium and saves us at the very last second. Otherwise, without that, we would kill with such ease. Half the
population would be dead. The way we're all so quick-tempered, we
would grab our gun and shoot down another person for no reason at
all. Look what happens with most people. Their murder weapon is
their car. They take out all their anger on it. On their car and on their
wife. They drive as if they wanted to kill the whole world. With a
vengeance. Repressed Freudian impulses. They say that Greek men
are confused about their sex life. Says who? I know one thing for
sure: Why are they all hanging around that square? Sure, there's
always Kyriakou Square or this square or that square, but I mean any
square at all. And all those men, what are they doing there? They're
hanging around trying to pick someone up from morning till night.
I can't understand it, when I think of my husband and all the women
he's slept with. My God, why such sexual hunger? I would have gotten sick of it. I swear to God, I would have been bored out of my
mind. It's not possible, something is very wrong with people. They
must be sick in the head. It's not possible to want to sleep with every
single woman who's even remotely attractive. How can some people
live like that? How is it possible to live with someone and not know
who he is? To think that you know him when he's hiding from you? To
conceal so many things? But is he really hiding them or are you just
imagining it? There he is, out somewhere sitting across from a young
woman, and it's such a lovely day he just can't help feeling a need to
put his hands on her, to touch her, and do all those other things to
her. All that is clear enough. I can understand it, but when it affects
me, when it causes me pain, I can't stand it. When it hurts me like
that. I understand it, it's very logical to want those privileges, especially if you're middle-aged, or older. But when the other person
can't take it? When it's so painful and difficult? I would like to be

different, a person with a lot of understanding. And in fact I am very understanding, but when it hurts me, I can't. I'm just not a martyr. The other mistake people make is that they don't keep anything hidden. They expose their innermost recesses. Living with someone makes you let yourself go and the other person learns everything about you. And that's disastrous, you lose yourself. What draws you to someone is the unknown. That quality you can never quite put your finger on. The impression that they're somehow keeping you at a distance. That there are regions which are forbidden to you. In which case I'm doomed from the start because I talk too much. I turn myself inside out, like a dress. Yesterday I cried for no reason. I was trying to get over this feeling of despair you get when you're a prisoner of circumstances you can't change. I don't like being humiliated. It's a terrible thing. You just can't accept it, especially not the way I was brought up. I see other women who can accept anything. Of course that leaves possibilities open to them. They aren't happy, but they aren't unhappy to such an extent. They don't fight back either, or how can I put it, resist, or fall down and die or lose all their hair. Or become nervous wrecks. The man is the boss, that's what they say. It's because that's the way they've been living since they were young, in that kind of atmosphere. That's the way their mothers lived. Nicole's mother-in-law didn't love the man she married, and she'd never been in love before she met him either. Then she had children and she never had time to think about it. And of course everyone keeps telling you: Why should that bother you, silly girl, aren't you Mrs. So-and-So? Ironclad logic. But all those old women are like that. And each one's son is always the best. Now really, what a lot of nonsense. I never believed that my son was the best. Not ever. The thought never even crossed my mind. Nor did I ever think he was handsome when he wasn't. I never thought he was anything. I just love him and that's all. And if he ever did any of the awful things that you men are always doing, I would probably be fighting with him from morning till night.

I would go and find him, talk to him, on my own initiative. I would tell him it just wasn't right to give someone else such a hard time. I would consider it my duty. I would try in every way I could to find a way to straighten things out between him and the woman he had married. Not go around saying ridiculous things about how my son is better than anyone else. Now, my second mother-in-law was like that. Exactly the same way; she had the same mentality. They all do. I wonder if they know—or if they try to convince themselves. They're obsessed with their children; they never love anyone else. Not the men who marry into the family, and not the women. It's always their daughters and their sons. Everyone else is an outsider. An enemy. It's terrible to think like that. And so very egotistical.

Maybe my nerves are shot, but this place is smothering me. All those people and so many cars around. When I go to London I relax. In America I felt refreshed. I love those tree-lined streets; I could walk for hours. Maybe because I'm away from my problems. I like to see new faces, new things. And to look at nice displays in store windows. I'm fascinated by things like that. The repetition around here is killing me. You go up to Kolonaki, you shop, you see the same old faces year after year in that square. The same old characters glued to the exact same chairs. They tire me, I just don't want them around anymore. All they do is talk, and they go on and on about me and about everybody else. It's really unbearable. I like being anonymous. I like to go and sit somewhere and have some woman or some man smile at me. On a bus; and I'll say something to them and they'll say something back. Little things. Even good-morning. But I can't do that here, because if you smile at someone they think that you're after something. And the women look at you as if you were out to steal their bag. That's just the way things are. It's terrible. They don't know how to be straightforward. They have a kind of mean look in their eyes. They peer at you out of the corner of their eyes, indirectly, and give you nasty looks. I don't like them. But I shouldn't be telling you things of such a personal nature. How do some foreigners manage to talk for hours without mentioning their own affairs? Have you noticed that? It's nice not to talk about yourself. To keep it all in. But if you keep it all in, one day it will all build up and you'll explode. Anyway, I discovered that my husband doesn't talk to me about anything but he does talk to other people on the telephone. What he talks about for hours and hours I can't understand. What can he be saying for so many hours to so many people? And when I ask him, of course, he doesn't reply. I don't think he's hiding anything. He just can't tell the truth. Because his truth is loneliness and he's afraid of it. And on top of it all there's this feeling of pity he has toward me, which is really intolerable. It infuriates me. One type of loneliness makes the other worse. I feel so hopeless when I see such a lack of maturity in the people around me. Where will it all end up? Where will it lead, this state of affairs? For God's sake. You see that something is not holding up, that something is giving way, and you don't make the slightest effort to prevent it. Why should two people not be able to tell the truth? You don't tell me anything either, since you never open your mouth. Maybe silence is your truth. You must be bored to death. It's as if every word had to be dragged out of you. The end result of total boredom. It could be the weather, because the weather affects all these things. It's getting worse and worse. Nobody picks up the telephone to call me anymore, and when I pick it up, I usually get myself into trouble. I'm probably incapable of keeping up many different relationships. Of playing that game. Well, if it is a game it's not worth much. I never saw anyone who cared when I had problems. With all the things that have happened to me lately. Everybody kind of disappeared. And that always made me feel very bad. Maybe it's my fault and I didn't try very hard to maintain my relationships. Out of tiredness. Out of boredom. Maybe my mistake is that I'm too wrapped up in myself. That I think I'm too important. More important than just one little person out of five billion. Then there's Gigi, who's so clever, so cultivated, with all her talent, but she's bored too. Mainly when there aren't men around. She only comes alive in the presence of men. Of course there are men who don't appeal to you, you're bored stiff with them. I have a friend, I love him, but I can't reach him. Certain things don't touch him. It's as if he were sealed off in a block of concrete and you keep pounding on it, hoping for some word, some message; and instead of that you come smack up against all these conventions. All those ideas about how you're supposed to be, how you should talk, how you should cross your legs. How a woman should treat her husband, how she should act in public. Ideas that are so rigid and inflexible they leave no room for thought. They just make you tired and you come out exhausted from the whole business.

Yesterday I was thinking of calling you and asking you to go out for dinner. Then I thought that I might not feel like talking, and then you would start saying: So what do we do now? Why don't I ever ask you that? I didn't feel like talking, I just felt like eating with you. Plain and simple. Everything is so simple. And so difficult. And you can't just start talking at any old time either. It depends on your mood, on your spirits. When I'm tired I keep losing my train of thought. I can't find the right words. And they have to come spontaneously, otherwise it's no good. Just to sit and think up things to tell you has no meaning. It's all meaningless anyway and I can't understand why you want me to tell you all these things. Look what a boor you are about it, too. That stubbornness of yours. Don't get angry. It's like when I tell you you're stupid. And when I tell a person they're stupid, whether it's a boyfriend of mine or a girlfriend of mine, I never mean they're stupid. You know what I mean. You use those expressions too. Everyone uses them. What's more, I can't hide anything. That's my weakness. Everyone tells me that's my greatest weakness. I can't hide what I'm feeling from people and I should have learned to. They took me to France before the war. How old was I

when I went? You see, I can hide that. I lived in France as a child and I
went to school there. Then I went to the Sudan. We took a big ship,
from Marseilles to Alexandria. We left Paris because there was a cri-
sis in the cotton industry and my father had to be near his work. I
told you he made his living from cotton. He and his brother used to
collect it and send it to Europe. That's how we left Paris. We got off
in Alexandria and I expected that on the wharf there would be lions
waiting to greet us. I believed that I would really see them and hear
them because all the books I used to read about Africa were filled
with them. Picture books, mainly. Some of the pictures are still very
vivid in my memory, and every now and then, for no reason, they pop
into my mind. Lions and palm trees, with those branches like
swords. I don't know if I liked that period very much. I didn't like
Alexandria. I never liked it, not even later when I was grown up and
lived there for a short time. I just had this feeling, this strong feeling,
that I was being drawn into something which wasn't going to be right
for me. Maybe because of my initial disappointment, which just
wouldn't go away, as if those lions still owed me something, even
though I had my grandmother there and she took very good care of
me. I used to live with her and she loved me very much. She had a
special fondness for me, although she did have another granddaugh-
ter and a grandson. He was killed in the war later on. In El Alamein,
I think. She had a real weak spot for me, but she also made my life
difficult sometimes. She would buy me all kinds of presents, and then
she would hide them all afterward. Expensive toys that were of no
use to me, since they ended up locked in some dark closet. She only
allowed me to take them out on Sundays. She would say: No, you
mustn't, because you'll break them. That was the way they thought,
those third-generation immigrants who had taken years and years to
amass their fortunes. She would say no about the toys, but then she
would change my teachers the minute I didn't get along with them.
I changed teachers quite a few times, and I vaguely remember one

who was Jewish. She was a Leo too. Grandma, not the teacher. I
found out by chance, after she had died when, years later, we had to
have her tombstone engraved. She died old too. In a certain way she
decided it was time to die, and she organized it all with a clear mind
and with resolve. As if she were going on vacation. What they should
dress her in, where and how they should bury her. She belonged to a
solid world; she was a product, you see, of a certain time, and her
death was no exception. Later, she sent for Ioasaph and shut herself
up with him, in her room, for four hours. She always called him just
plain Ioasaph. She showed him her indulgence in that way, and they
were very good friends. She supported various foundations of his.
And when the Patriarch finally came out of there he looked overwhelmed. He crossed himself, made a cross in the air behind him,
and ran out like a thief, without a word. She hadn't called him for her
last confession as he had thought, and she had badgered him with
questions for four hours. It took her four hours to get around his
objections: Since something like that was done two or three hundred
years ago, it could be done now. But you see she was the daughter of
merchants and the mother of merchants and bargaining was in her
blood. That same afternoon a young canon with a red beard from the
Patriarchate appeared and presented her with a sealed sheet of parchment. He didn't stay very long; he handed over the parchment to her
and left immediately, carrying a goat's-hair bag on his back with five
thousand Victorian crowns minted in the year 1900. All that according to Uncle Aristides' testimony. Two days later they buried her. In
her clasped hands, instead of the small icon of the Resurrection, they
had placed a braided silver purse from her wedding. In that purse,
along with the official certificate of absolution from her sins, were
the fourteen umbilical cords of the children she had given birth to.
Fourteen hard, shriveled cords, like discarded old springs. Isn't that
macabre? She had given birth to fourteen children but only six of
them had survived, and now she was taking them with her, those

shriveled cords she had saved, wrapped in a bit of cotton, inside a piece of faded satin. Maybe as tokens of her identity. Still, I would have liked to have been like her. To have inherited her nerve. Unfortunately I didn't, and since that time I've seen her twice in my dreams. It was at no time in particular, when I had completely forgotten about her. In the first dream her age was not clear to me, but it was before I was born. That is, she was young. She was waiting somewhere, and she was holding, carelessly and slightly at a slant, on her right shoulder, a summer umbrella made out of printed material. There was no sun and the place must have been the train station at Piraeus. Not exactly, but it looked a lot like it, because up above there were those huge glass skylights that filtered out the afternoon light. She was walking slowly along the deserted quays, and she was waiting, holding her open umbrella. She was wearing a light dress and silk stockings, and the scent of her skin created an aura of freshness in the midst of the silence. Because naturally there was a dead silence, a complete absence of sound. Maybe even a complete absence of gravity. It was a wait without an end but with an erotic certainty to it. In the other dream she was helping me get ready to leave on vacation for Khartoum. It was all taking place in my room, and I was ten years old, but the strange thing was that there were two of me in the dream because I was conscious of the fact that I was having a dream. And I was aware that a lot of time had passed in the meantime. So there I was watching myself getting ready, all impatient. I was always impatient when it was time to leave for Khartoum. It had become a tradition to spend a few weeks a year there with my parents. They used to take me there when school was over. It was nice there, but it was also boring. Days upon uneventful, blank days when I didn't know what to do with myself. And they also used to keep me quite confined, even though I was still way under the age of puberty. My father believed that a girl should get married and have children, that that was her destiny and nothing else. Those were his ideas, our code of behavior,

which was in force for everyone, except for my mother. He adored
my mother, he had a real weakness for her, and she did whatever she
pleased with him. She exercised some strange charm over him, and
even though he was difficult and something of a tyrant in his youth,
or so they say, he had a need to let her have her way with him, he
needed her to dominate him. When they were together they were so
close to one another that I always felt left out. I don't know, perhaps
her being there perpetually excited him and he didn't have eyes for
me. However, when she went away, and she went away often and left
us alone, we got on very well, the two of us. Then they sent me to
that nun's school, Notre Dame De Sion, for three years, in Cairo.
And I think that did me a lot of harm. After Grandma died, they took
me to Cairo so that I could be closer to them. I mean closer in distance. Ten or twenty kilometers away, that is. They sent me to board-
ing school with those nuns, and I was only allowed to come out on
weekends. They had arranged for me to spend weekends at the home
of some friends of theirs. The couple were friends of my mother's and
the husband was the president of the Greek Community—a very
prominent family. But I shouldn't mention any names. They had two
sons; one was about my age, the other was a baby, and one of the first
times I went there, we were sitting around, and their father asked me
to go and get a film from somewhere so we could show it. I went to
get the film from some room, which was piled up with all kinds of
things, like a storeroom, and as soon as I walked in the door the son
was there and he grabbed me. He took hold of my breast, even
though I was still not fully developed, and he put his other hand on
my thigh, and he kissed me right on the mouth. Passionately and
furtively. And then I went completely out of my mind. I was still very
young, maybe thirteen or fourteen. I don't remember. Of course I
told my mother immediately, because she could see it on my face that
something had happened which had upset me tremendously. And
after that everything changed. They no longer allowed me to leave

school, because I guess they thought that if I came out on weekends, he would not only kiss me but would do other things to me. The father was not only short and fat, he was bald and old. His wife had married him out of necessity, because she had no money, and later on, when she was widowed, she remarried almost immediately. She was pretty and much younger than he was, almost twenty years. Her other son, the baby—what a strange coincidence—came and rented the penthouse across the way. The one on the corner across the street from me, when it was changing tenants, and he died last year at the age of thirty-six. Isn't that strange? All the way from Cairo and he ends up living across from me again, after so many years. So much for the other son. I don't know if he ever found out that we were neighbors; I had changed my name then, for the third time. Anyway, after that I never went back to their house again. I wasn't allowed out of school anymore and all that was left was study, prayer, and church. You have no idea what Catholics are like. So, even though my childhood was quite happy, and in all the photographs of me I look cheerful enough, later on I became melancholic. Being confined like that was very bad for me, and perhaps it gave me the wrong idea about life. Everything was a great sin. Everything. They even used pieces of tape to censor books. Books by authors like Mme Delu, for example, which are the most harmless books you can imagine. Whenever there were young people falling in love or kissing, they would put a piece of tape there, and we would sneak the books into our dormitories and hold them up against the light, trying to find those kisses along the edge of the tape. No, it wasn't our wanton nature; it was normal, natural curiosity. We didn't do anything either. I don't know about the other girls, but I didn't anyway. I don't know about the nuns either and what they did. One of them might have been a lesbian. Maybe, because this friend of mine, Catherine, told her parents that she used to fondle her. She would touch her and everything. At which time a scandal broke out, but what was going on between them I

don't know. Maybe nothing was going on. But I never did the thing
you talked about, no. At least not then. An act of need. You put it
well; but it could also have been an act of loneliness, because I tried it
later on. Much later and under different circumstances. For no reason in particular. Because I was bored and fed up with everything.
The only trouble is that it doesn't bring you happiness. It simply
relieves you. You quiver for a moment, as if your cells were being
split in two, lost in their own darkness, and then you feel completely
empty and even less than what you were before. Such despair. But I
might be mistaken about all this. I don't know. It could just be
because of the problems I've always had. Because although I discovered sex when I was practically in kindergarten, I made love for the
first time quite late. Late even by the standards of my own genera-
tion. In Italy with someone who I'm not sure I liked. Really, I didn't
like him and I had just turned twenty-three. That first time which
they say makes such an impression on you. Nonsense. For me it was a
decision I made quite rationally and no trace of it has remained with
me. No emotion, or even the memory of one. Not even a shock, like
with my tooth, for instance. The first tooth I had to have fixed, and it
was at about the same time. I had a cavity. And I don't mean I was
afraid of the drilling or of the pain, because it didn't hurt at all, and
anyway I had to have other teeth fixed after that. I mean that strange
feeling that lasted for about a month. It was the first "crack" and, even
though it had been restored so painlessly, for several days my tongue,
irritated, kept sliding back to that spot, again and again. Irritated and
annoyed by the inert foreign matter that had wedged itself into my
body, but it had also wedged itself into my being, like the thorn of a
prickly pear, and it took me a month to forget it. I don't know. And
all this is so private. I don't know if I'm a very sensual person. I have
to love someone to be able to function. And now it's like the cycle has
finally come full swing and I have so many fillings. In the end, it
seems to me that there were only two people who made any kind of

impression on my life. One of them many years later. The first one was in Africa. We used to go out all together in the evening. There was this family who were all friends of ours. They were a nice family. They knew how to have a good time and they had a lot of freedom. They were all good-looking, they had very nice bodies, and every night they had people at their house—every single night. I was seventeen and very shy, so much so that one day I fell in the pool. I was walking along and I was so self-conscious that I fell in the pool and I felt really bad, because they were used to having their freedom and they didn't seem to be weighed down by all these complexes. And, yes, I really liked him. Maybe not in the beginning. He had been after me for a long time and I didn't want to. Then things changed and I did want to. Anyway, we flirted, completely innocently that is, and one night he took me back to school, and he kissed me. I was seventeen and I wanted him, but in spite of all that I was so terribly upset that all night long I bit my pillow in anger, and secretly I felt disgust, can you imagine that? A terrible loathing, even though I wanted him, because that's the way I'd been programmed to be, the way my mind worked. Anyway, I discovered sex on a beach in Brittany. Every August my mother and I went to Brittany, and all along the beach there were striped tents, like in that film *Death in Venice*. There are some photographs, but I have to look for them in some old trunk somewhere. That's where I discovered sex. There was a young boy, the son of some friends of my mother, and we were alone behind some cabins. I knew a few things by then, of course. They had sent me to a school that was also a sort of finishing school for older girls. American and English girls mainly. How or why I went to that school I don't remember. I only remember that everyone liked me a lot. I was like their mascot. I remember the fat cook whose name was Josephine, and whenever she made crepes she would call me into the kitchen and would let me be the first to taste them. Chubby old Josephine with her big bosom, her plump white arms, and that glow-

ing smile of hers. Even when she was angry she glowed. She would
beat the batter, drop some in the pan, and then toss it up high, way up
high, and back down it would come right into the pan; it was such a
miraculous feat. Josephine, like some cheerful goddess, forever
filling those crepes with jam and wrapping them up. And the headmistress of the school liked me too. She was an Englishwoman of
Russian origin, about my mother's age, a little taller, and she had
traveled quite a bit. But where she had traveled to I still couldn't
understand. Anyway, to Africa for certain, because she had ostrich
eggs in her room and she used to take me up there often. She had a
lot of other things, small glass objects in glass cases, and she used to
let me play with them. Some were colored, with pictures on them,
and it was a very beautiful world there among all those strange
objects. One day she made some drawings for us on the blackboard,
showing that in order to have children certain things have to happen.
On the blackboard with chalk. And afterward, when we were
finished, I went running home and told everyone all about it, full of
enthusiasm, of course. Then my mother, outraged, went straight to
school that very minute, and there was a tremendous fuss with the
headmistress. Anyway, so there I was with that young boy behind
those cabins, and I said to him: Pull down your pants right now so I
can see what you look like down there. I remember, the tents and the
beach and the young boy—more or less. He pulled down his pants
and I put my hand there and touched him.

   My God, what a story. Why did I remember it now? Now I
don't feel the least bit curious. About anything. No enthusiasm. I no
longer enjoy sitting in the sun. Sitting with people. I don't know. I
have such a feeling of…I'm ashamed. I feel humiliated. It's as though
everybody knows, as though I've become transparent, as though they
can see inside me. And it's so unpleasant. But that's just plain stupid,
it's foolish oversensitivity. And I talk too much. It's the loneliness
syndrome, I guess. I had lunch a few days ago with Loukas, a child-

hood friend from Alexandria. I hadn't seen him for four years. He called and said let's get together, and we went to one of those tavernas in Thision. Where they have those wax-paper tablecloths that have become such a part of Athenian folklore. I had a few drinks, and I talked for three hours straight. I didn't let him get a word in edgewise. I think I drove him crazy with all that talking. Now he won't call me for another four years. Pepi, who also never stops talking, insists that she doesn't even come close to me. And her husband, every time he comes into the house and we're on the phone, starts to whistle. As if to say: Come on, finish up. Then he really starts to get worried about a phone call going on for such a long time between his two wives. Oh yes, I'm his ex-wife and she's his second wife. He starts whistling like this, impatiently, to see when we'll get tired and stop. In France they used to put me in a highchair, one of those chairs with beads for very young children. It had beads and in the front was a wooden tray, and they put me up there and I would watch the others eating at lunchtime. My aunt, who was French, used to say: Children should be seen but not heard. I've never forgotten those words. Children should be seen but not heard. So I wasn't supposed to talk at all. Everyone else would eat and talk, and I would sit there watching them. All that in a castle, near Bordeaux. My uncle lived there, the one who was married to that French woman. The castle belonged to her, in fact. It had large rooms with large beds. Everything was big except for me. Beds with baldaquins, the kind with four posts and painted canopies. With curtains, too. Beds like tombs. And then, because I was thin, they would tell me that if I didn't eat, the bogeyman would come. They tried unsuccessfully to convince me that that was why I should eat. It was an approach that was clearly misguided. There were a lot of theories like that in those days. They would take me upstairs to bed, and someone would wear a sheet and pretend to be the bogeyman. I don't know who, but I could always hear a pan banging. I would get frightened, all alone in that big bed. There was also a big window there. And I would listen all night to those loud, banging noises and get so scared. But I didn't eat more because of all that. My stubbornness prevailed and I refused to give in. And then there was a door. It separated a long corridor with a high ceiling from some kitchen that was no longer in use. I never went through that door, and it has remained in my mind as a threshold of terror. In spite of all that, I liked the castle. We spent several weeks there every spring, and I had a wonderful doll that I forgot there once. I asked them to look for it, but by the time I realized it, it was too late. They never sent it back to me. Those were the most important years of my life. Of course, they were also very lonely years, but it was a different kind of loneliness. Back then when I cried I would wake up feeling fine. Because I didn't have to justify anything to myself and because my happiness or my unhappiness depended exclusively on others. Now it's not like that anymore. Now I wake up with swollen eyes and my mind dulled by disuse. You'd think my head was filled with fog. I don't want time to keep passing. It's like I've been thrown into a well and I'm trying to get out into the sun, but I just can't make it. So much effort all in vain. I can't fall back on my childhood years anymore either. Or rather, even that has become a kind of sickness. I've always lived in pleasant surroundings, and everything was much bigger than in real life. Like with my toys, when I saw them again later on and felt slightly disappointed. I used to go out with Beatrice, and she had long hair. She always wore one of those large-rimmed, curvy hats made out of *feutre*—what's that soft material called again, "felt"? I can't remember the word for it. She used to take me out, and I had a big crush on the coal merchant's son. Of course no one wanted me to be hanging around with the coal merchant's son. I don't remember what his name was, I don't remember his face; I only remember that at home they used to tease me: *Elle est très amie avec le fils du bougnat.* *Bougnat* is a slang word for coal merchant. Whenever I went out he'd be there at the corner. They would dress me in a red coat and red

stockings and shoes with straps and a red woolen cap. I remember it
all so vividly, wearing all those things, and never any gloves. I would
never wear gloves even though my parents insisted. The loneliness
syndrome. But what is loneliness anyway? Perhaps the end result of a
bad life. When I was younger I could have put up with such things.
There are some days when I feel like I'm a thousand years old. When
I feel so weighed down I just can't go on. Now I get tired easily. And I
get bored. I don't enjoy myself anymore the way I did before. Just
going out in the morning and having a brand new day ahead of you.
Looking up at the sky with all its promises. And reading a book or
seeing a friend. All those things. I don't know, maybe it's because
emotionally I'm always in such a state of turmoil. Back then there
were days when I used to feel so light. Now nothing has any interest
for me. All I feel is loneliness pouring over me, seeping into my body
and through my flesh, like a low fever. No matter where I go there
comes a moment when it simply overwhelms me and then I say: Why
all of this, what good is it, what's the use? I don't think that it's
because I'm getting on in years. I don't think that it's a matter of age.
It's the sum total of a bad life. I'm simply unhappy. Maybe for no reason at all, and I'm just not capable of seeing beauty. Perhaps I do see it
sometimes, but so fleetingly, as if it were nothing more than a
reflection. And I also wish that people were more accessible, but
they're not. They all have their jobs, their families, their problems,
and they don't have time. Once I used to read a lot. Now I don't read
at all. Especially since the time when I began to feel so disturbed deep
down inside. I can't concentrate on any book. Years ago I used to read
for hours. I would lie in bed reading, suffused with pleasure, and I
would feel good just being myself. Now I don't ever feel good, not
anywhere. The sum total of a bad life. But then again, I think that I
could have been worse off. I could have had some terrible disease, or
something could have happened to my children, or as they say here in
Greece: Terrible calamities could have befallen me. I could have gone

to jail or gone blind, or any number of things. I don't know. I can't
understand why it has to be like this. As though there were a wild animal inside you, and you say: Why me, I had such dreams and wanted
so much, why should it all be ending? But it's wrong to think the way
I do. So many things all wrong. And very egotistical. Perhaps people
should accept themselves and make their peace with themselves. But
how can you come to terms with all the things that are tearing you
apart? I don't want to generalize, because it may be only me who
feels this way, because my life is such a mess. Maybe if I were happy.
And I know how easy it would be for me to be happy. But when you
think about the fact that all the things you wanted can never happen,
then what, what's left? You always say: I'm young, I have time.
Tomorrow or some other time, next week, next month, there's
plenty of time. And finally you arrive at a point when you realize that
there isn't any time left. And that's what drives you really crazy.
Maybe that's why I feel like this all the time, as though I were living in
a dream. Not a dream, now it's a nightmare.

When I was little I had one of those kaleidoscopes where you
put your eyes up close and see pictures moving around. They used to
give me so many presents every Christmas. I would leave my stockings by the fireplace and while I was sleeping they would fill them
with gifts. I knew that Santa Claus didn't really exist, but that in no
way lessened the enchantment. They would fill them with gifts, and
my tree as well. They always put up a tall tree for me that reached all
the way up to the sky. Or rather, the ceiling. And they decorated it
with all kinds of lovely things. They weren't made out of paper or
plastic, like they are today. They were real porcelain. Porcelain ballerinas hanging from the branches and boats pulled by swans. Those
toys must be very valuable today because they don't make them anymore. Unfortunately, because we moved so often and traveled so
much I didn't save them. Ballerinas that looked so real, with those
skirts, tutus, made out of yellow gauze. Canary yellow that shone in

the dark. My room had a radiator, but it also had a fireplace, and on the coldest days of winter they would light a fire in it. I would get into bed and the flames would flicker all night long, and the scenes on my wallpaper would come alive. That wallpaper had so many different scenes. That *toile de Jouy*, like in the old days. A story by La Fontaine. There was a witch with her high hat, high and pointed, riding along on her broom. There she was, that witch and her children, right there in my room. They would dance around, and it was all projected over and over again on the wall by the flames. It was a crazy dance, and I would pull the sheet up to my eyes and gaze into the night, afraid. All that was like a fairy tale. That's why I keep saying that I haven't grown up and that I'm stuck back there. Me and all those beautiful toys of mine. But then I used to sleep, in spite of all my fears, and in the morning I would draw lines across the windowpane to wipe away the mist and see what was happening across the way. It was always all covered in snow, well, usually. Then Beatrice would take me out. We would go to Muette. We would go to the Bois de Boulogne. I have a photograph of the two of us. I'm sitting on her lap, in the sun, in the Bois de Boulogne, and I have bangs. They used to sell those *cerceaux* then. They were large wooden hoops with a stick, and you would hit them and they would roll forward and you would run after them. I don't know what use they were, but everyone liked them. I also had roller skates. There were large, tree-lined paths for children only and we all had roller skates. Anyway, when I had my own twins and they reached a certain age, I told them that I knew how to skate very well. We had rented a house in Glyfada for the summer. I made them sit up on a wall, and I brought my skates to show them. I put them on, started to go really fast, and fell, of course, because it had been so many years since I'd last tried to skate. I fell and hurt myself badly. I hit my forehead, and they thought it was all just terrific. They were both so little. I used to dress them in corduroy overalls with crossing straps. They were all enthusiastic, clapping their hands and shouting: Hooray for Mama, hooray for Mama. And there I was in agony, dying of pain from that fall, and my poor eye was black and blue for twenty days. Because if you hit yourself on the forehead, that purplelike color spreads down your face, and I looked just like a corpse for the next twenty days. I kept looking at myself in the mirror and getting so scared. I was terrified by the color of my bruised flesh. Especially when it began to spread from my eyes down toward my nose. I felt as if death itself was in combat with Hades and was slowly creeping up on me. Isn't that a crazy idea? Death and Hades in combat. Of course, the way you're afraid of death is different when you're twenty-five from what it is now. Today I'm not really afraid at all. Not because I've become brave, but because it's always there. You get used to it, and that's the worst thing of all. Like lightning in a rainstorm, which is another thing I've become used to. It doesn't send shivers up my spine anymore, or make my knees tremble. It could be that my fear was due to something more than just my associating that purplelike color with death. I didn't want to look at myself in the mirror, but I couldn't help it. And one morning I realized for a fleeting moment how much I looked like my mother. That likeness—which lasted so briefly, only for a moment, and which I had never noticed before, nor did I ever see it again after that—seemed, without my knowing why, like a bad omen. Because my mother and I are completely different from one another. So, of course, it was an omen of something that hasn't happened yet, although when it comes right down to it, it could all be connected to my childhood traumas. Unlike me, she was a strong character. She still is, in spite of her seventy-odd years. When I was young she would only allow me to give her a kiss or ask me for one, depending on the case, when she herself wanted to. Eventually, because of the constraints she imposed on me, I began to find her so repulsive that I didn't want to kiss her. It annoyed me when she made me kiss her; I didn't want to touch her skin; I didn't want her to caress me.

I always wanted to reach out my hands and just push her away. Much later, in recent years, once or twice when I was having problems, I hugged her but I felt ashamed of my weakness. I was ashamed of having done it, and I knew that deep down she would never really understand why I was upset or how superficial it all was. It was at moments like that that she would tell me: You see how much I love you and how much I've done for you and how many sacrifices I've made for the family. The same old refrain all the time, about all her sacrifices. I don't know whether she made sacrifices or not, but in the end I was the one left dangling in midair. I don't know, perhaps I'm mistaken, but her kisses never had any tenderness to them. I always felt there was something cold about that woman. We haven't seen each other for nine months, because we quarrel often, and we stop seeing each other for long periods of time, and then there are moments when I go looking for her. I know that she will never take the first step, and of course I won't go and see her either. And I know that, even if I do go, we'll end up fighting again and we still won't understand anything about each other. Then I keep thinking that one day she'll be even older. What can you do? She never accepted me and she still doesn't accept me. Everything is always all my fault, and whenever my daughter does something wrong, she always says: You're just like your mother. I mean when it's something that my mother thinks is wrong. And that habit she has of talking to absolutely everyone about me, about how I did this and how I did that, something which has bothered me incredibly since I was a child. She has this compulsion to talk about things. She has this way of distorting the truth, like telling you that you've spent a fortune when you haven't really spent anything. And all that because once I had some shares of stock that were worth eighty drachmas each and I sold a thousand of them, so that I could get eighty thousand drachmas. She kept accusing me of throwing seven million drachmas down the drain, because the stock later passed on to new owners, to another company, and one day its value went up. Things like that. Saying that I spend too much money, which is a lie, or that I changed my curtains ten times, when I only changed them twice. All I did was put up some curtains and because I didn't really like them I put up some new ones. Silly little things like that. Anyway, I had the means to do it, and besides, it was my house and my money. Or that I had my wooden floors refinished five times, which is also a lie. It was just that the floorboards were defective, they were painted with this awful varnish, so I had it scraped off. Wherever she goes that's all she talks about. She goes on and on about what I did, which is always wrong. And that bothers me; it really bothers me. I wonder why things have to be like this. Maybe she didn't want me, or she didn't like me from the moment she had me. Maybe she would have preferred a boy. She would often tell me: You were beautiful but I never was. And I can understand that, but she was clever. She wasn't beautiful, by our standards today, but she had an air about her, and because she was always well-dressed and, of course, younger, she would walk into a place and you would notice her immediately. You couldn't ignore her. But beautiful, no, she never was. She had a rather angular face, with that sharp, chiseled look, which was her charm and her strength. That and her strong, thin legs. And now she's old. She's no longer even a shadow of her former self. Her body's just not what it used to be. But she's still strong. Then again, maybe it's all self-defense. It could always have been self-defense, simply hidden despair, that hardness of hers. Maybe it's all in my head, all this, I don't know. There are moments when it's so painful for me to see the way she looks hanging there in that portrait of her in her prime. It was done in 1928 or '29 in Italy, and the man who painted it was a very good artist. I think it has the date on it. It was done around the same time as one of me holding my first bulldog in my arms. That portrait has done quite a bit of traveling, but my second husband sent it to me packed all wrong. Instead of the good side facing out it was facing in, and it was sent to Zurich through some mistake of the company and came back smashed to bits. I sent it out to be repaired. That was ten years ago. Fifteen years ago. I asked where I could find an art restorer, and they told me about someone who restored icons. He was very well known. The only thing was he hadn't the slightest idea about anything other than icons, and as I was very busy then because I was going abroad, I left it with him, and when I came back he had destroyed it. Because he'd taken its white satin backdrop and made it ivory. And he ruined my mother's fur coat, too. He changed the way the fur looked, and it came out too smooth in the end. Only the face remained unchanged. But that white in the background, which gave it so much brightness, was gone. Anyway, it's really painful for me to see her looking so defensive, even if it is just a painting. Maybe that's why I felt so afraid. I don't know. At any rate, the repairs were paid for by the airline company that had been responsible for the mix-up. But what difference does it make? I often remember how she looked when she was young. I liked the way she dressed and the way she was always so pleasant to other people. With all the things she knew she could carry on quite a conversation, and do so many other things, too. But she was forever saying: My daughter is pretty, I'm not. In that coy sort of way she had. But it was always with just the slightest note of complaint, and you could never quite tell if she was serious or not. And because of that it was all the more poignant. But there was also something else she used to say: That daughter of mine. She could have done so many things and yet she never did anything with her life. It was a thorn in her flesh that I'd never done anything and that I'd never made the kind of marriages she would have liked me to. And she was right, in spite of the fact that I don't agree with her. Because I really didn't do anything; I didn't even make the kind of marriage that I myself would have wanted, the three times I was married. And I suppose all that was my reaction to an authoritarian life, however ridiculous it may now seem for me to say so. Of course I may have been born that way. Have had something in my blood, some sort of peasant strain, not peasant, something else from some distant relative or other that would be better forgotten. Some sort of family disgrace. Like one of my dogs later on who turned out, in spite of all her certificates and pedigrees, not to be a pure breed. And why she was not has always remained a mystery, at least to me. Maybe it was one of nature's caprices. So many maybes. When it comes right down to it, we are all of us a mystery, aren't we? And each one of us has an opinion about himself and about everyone else. One person sees another as delightful and nice, another one sees him as awful, a liar and so on, a third person sees him I don't know how, and a fourth one is careful of what he says, and in the end you have such a strange mixture. Unless of course you're perfect, if you've never made a mistake, not when it comes to your marriages or to other important decisions and everything has turned out just right for you. As far as I'm concerned, however, nothing has turned out right and I don't know what people out there think of me, but I don't care either. The only thing that concerns me is that from a certain time onward I've had this feeling of loneliness, whereas before I was never alone. There were always people around me, I would talk continuously—but to other people, not like now, and that may have been foolish of me, but it didn't make me feel so bogged down and depressed. And I used to love traveling. Especially when I was meeting someone at the other end. Back then I'd be full of enthusiasm whenever someone told me to get on a plane or in a car or in anything at all that was going somewhere. And I used to drive for hours on end. I was crazy about it, I'd drive for ten or twelve hours. I'd take the car and drive off somewhere; I'd go to Kavala, for example, and I'd stop for twenty minutes along the way to have a coffee and then I'd continue. Like that for nine or ten hours. I loved it. Now I can't do it, it makes me tired. Not physically, it tires me psychologically. Or rather, I can't be bothered. I used to like trains also. Not boats. They were much too slow for me, and all that sea day after day used to sap my energy. I wonder if maybe all that running around was nothing more than an attempt to escape from myself. If so, then that was why I didn't like boats. Because they're so slow that your self catches up with you and you can't just jump into the sea and escape, of course, because then you'll drown. And now here we are again, tête-à-tête, just my self and me, and with such dismal prospects ahead. Such a strange cycle. In Khartoum, the second time I was there, I had this French governess, well, actually she was from the Levant. I used to tell her: I know that I'll end up alone, I feel it. She would start shouting: You're crazy, you're only sixteen years old, how can you believe such a thing? I have no idea why I used to think like that. And in the end I did wind up alone. Now it could be that all people are alone, but I'm even more alone. They tell me: You have your children, what more could you want? It's nice to have children, but my children will go away. They have their own life, so why should they be concerned with me? And I'm not just some woman you can bring to live in your house either, someone you can shut in a room and have her sneak out like a mouse whenever you haven't any company. And I wouldn't like to end up like Aigle either. No one helped her during those crucial years. She tried to help herself, she had the will. But she went through it all in a state of unimaginable loneliness. I think of her often lately. They treated her so ungratefully, not ungratefully, that's the wrong word. That son of hers used to go round there, and he was usually so indifferent; he would sit there snoring at the table and he never listened to her, and he was rude and nasty to her. And Artemis, who's so sensitive and bright, used to tell me: I can't take her, I just can't take her. Even Maurice, who used to come with her, I mean Artemis's boyfriend, said the same thing: Oh, that Aigle, she's a crazy one. But Aigle would do absolutely anything for her children. We would go out and she would talk about them for hours on end. She lived in an apartment, a penthouse of course, a nice bright one, even though she had a mag-

nificent old house on Herodotou Street, which she had to sell. Or
rather, she leased it to a contractor who built offices there, and she
would send all the rent she collected from them to her children in
Europe. And all they could say was: Oh, that mother of ours; well,
after all, she still has the villa in Magoufana. And they made her life
unbearable. I have a painting of hers at home which is like a nightmare. Really, she was always painting things like that. Hers was a
cruel world, she was always so troubled. I have that painting in the
hall, as you come in on the right, a painting done in deep blue, almost
black. It's of two heads from the shoulders up, embracing each other,
and they look kind of like embryos. Artemis brought it to me on one
of her brief visits from abroad for her mother's annual memorial service. Oh, those pangs of conscience every summer. At any rate, after
Aigle died, her house in Magoufana was left, and Artemis called me
from Geneva to ask how to go about renting it, it was in such a
wretched state. So I took on the job and imagine, something like that
could only happen to me. Only to me, it couldn't possibly happen to
anyone else. I put up advertisements, I ran around showing it to people, but nobody wanted it because it had such an unusual layout.
Aigle was both a bohemian and an artist, a little of each, and the
house had everything except bedrooms. It had a studio, it had a
garage, it had a pool with a fountain to water the garden, only it had
no bedrooms. A lot of people came to see it, but they would all say:
Thank you, but without any bedrooms it's just not what we want.
And in the end who did I find? This man who owned a zoo. He kept
lions and some other animals, out at some villa in Ano Patissia. He
got in touch with me and I remembered him, that is, it turned out we
knew each other through somebody else. I knew his brother; he was
once director of t.a.e., the company that later became Olympic
Airlines. He also had snakes and God only knows what else. Anyway,
I phoned Artemis in Geneva and I told her: Listen, I put it in the
newspapers; a lot of people called me and came to see it, but the only

one seriously interested is this man. So Artemis gave me her answer, all the way from Geneva, the heart of civilization and everything, and what did she answer: Well, Maria, do whatever you want, but not someone with lions in my mother's house, she said. How can we do such a thing, it's just not right. And I just kept thinking that a thing like that could only happen to me. To find a tenant who had wild animals. Anyway, I decided to go and see him. He lived in Patissia in a villa, and he had a license and he kept insisting: I have a permit from the police, so why should it bother anyone. Aigle would have liked the idea of lions in her garden. Artemis never agreed to it.

She was so unpredictable and so full of life. And now there is no Aigle. I think of her often, and it makes me mad to think that everything must come to an end. I don't know. Just the thought that someday I won't be here either. I don't care if I live to a ripe old age or if I ever become a grandmother and all that. I really don't care. What consolation can that be? Because by then everything will be falling apart, I won't be strong, and since I already look at things like this today, how will I look at them later on? And that drives me crazy. I met Mrs. Brückmann in the street the day before yesterday, and I said that we should go to the movies one of these days. I was trying to be nice to her. She's old and she's alone. And of course she drinks. Maybe I said that to her out of self-pity, maybe I was projecting my own feelings onto her. She laughed kind of like this: *ha ha*, and didn't give me an answer. I realized that meant we weren't going to the movies. She's German and has remained a German, although she was born here. I mean one of those tough German women. Like my mother, but my mother is Mediterranean. Anyway, I don't believe that such traits are determined by nationality. It's simply the virtue of having endured. Of being eighty years old and saying *ha ha ha*, like Mrs. Brückmann. Her only son is now living in Algiers, and she's alone. Like me, with three marriages behind her and various lovers in between. Now there's someone who was way ahead of her time. But one has to pay for all that, you see. When you break with tradition, when you can't put up with it, not put up with it, when you get sick and tired of following in the same old footsteps. It's almost like a punishment of some sort, because you refused to give in. And once you've refused the first time, you'll continue to refuse until the end. You can't possibly go back to the comfort of a family. What family, anyway? Once there used to be proper families. There were grandparents, aunts and uncles, grandchildren, and that gave meaning to everyone's life. Today there are no big families anymore, there aren't even houses, there are only apartments and they keep on getting smaller; they aren't high and spacious anymore, and they're so confining. And everything has become so expensive. Old people are put in those terrible institutions, on which they have the nerve to write Home for the Aged, for the white-haired. But how can they just reduce you to nothing like that? The mansion of Anargyros Moudros on Chios used to be quite a hotel, so they say. Even though he chose to leave in the end. Whereas I would have left right from the beginning. He gave it all up when he was sixty, his income, the hotel, the servants, the chambermaids, and all the rest, and went to Mount Athos to become a monk. To save his soul, because he had filled the island with illegitimate children. Just like that. Maybe I got his chromosomes, but with the code all scrambled. Maybe that's the reason I'm so bothered by being alone. Because I would always run away, even from the things I loved, and from the people too, and I never stopped to look myself straight in the eye. And the men I loved, I couldn't stick it out with them for long either. Especially P. He was crazy in those days, not only about me, about everything. He was quite an exuberant character, always exploding like a volcano, and every time we got together we would have a great time, for about half an hour. Then I would start getting annoyed because he used to run his fingers through my hair and tug at my clothing and that bothered me. In those days I was still a very neat person and he would ask

me: Why do you keep fixing your hair like that?; everybody runs
their fingers through someone's hair sometimes, it's only natural and
it's okay. Today, of course, I wouldn't care at all, but back then, in the
fifties, we used to use hair spray and do our hair up in those high bee-
hives and that would mess it up, and the idea of being disorderly
bothered me. How stupid. I discovered the secret of nice hair later on
when I cut it. And P. He was like a whirlwind, all the time, that's just
the way he was. Everything had to be done in a burst of enthusiasm,
without stopping, quickly. It was like being on a roller coaster that
turned you upside down over and over again. We would start out
together in the morning, and by the end of the day we could barely
drag ourselves round. There were so many hours, so many places, so
many people in his world, that by the next morning I'd be completely
exhausted. I couldn't take it anymore, that pace day in and day out,
and I'd find myself saying: When will it ever stop? We ate too much,
we drank too much, we talked too much, we ran around too much,
and there was always someone, without fail, who would turn up and
drag us somewhere else. Because P. couldn't say no to anyone and he
loved being with people. So around and around we went, from one
place to another, all day long, twenty-four hours a day. In the meantime I used to love chocolate, and I still do, but it was bad for my
liver, so every once in a while I'd have an attack, and then I'd have to
follow him around in all that discomfort and pain. Today, of course,
I can laugh about it because my doctor has forbidden me to eat
chocolate, but back then I would curse and I'd say: My God, let me go
somewhere and find some peace and quiet. And I would leave. I
would get on the train and leave, just to get away from it all and from
him, too. I would come back feeling much better, but before I could
even unpack my suitcase, Iris would already have sent a telegram saying: Send her back. Iris was a friend of ours, a friend of mine and a
friend of P.'s, and she was our own special postal service. Iris had
these fantastic blue eyes, and the three of us used to have the greatest

times together. Because of that quality she had of being able to pre-
serve the image of everything beautiful reflected in her eyes. So I
would wait a few days, until I had recovered and felt like leaving
again, and I would get back on the plane or the train, full of enthusiasm, and off I'd go again. All over again, right from the beginning. On
and off it went like that for a year and a half. There was no escape, and
I finally took a house there, to save at least some part of my travel
expenses and to avoid the bother of going back and forth. I rented
that house by myself, without his knowing it, and I thought that I was
renting an apartment, but as I didn't understand the language well, it
turned out that I had to share it with the woman who owned it. And
when I walked in and started unpacking my things, she appeared
from some room in the back, and when I asked her what she was
doing there, she said: I live here. She showed me her typewriter and
some papers, but whatever was written in them I never found out.
Anyway, she used to write for hours and she rarely came out of her
cubbyhole, only at mealtime. After a while we became sort of
friendly, and she told me that in her youth she had had many lovers
and that her hair had been reddish-blond back then. She was fat and
ugly but nice. Very nice, and she had this habit of pinning up notes for
me all over the place. She would even pin them up in midair, on the
lights, or on the lampshades, but she never left them on the table, it
was really strange. Notes that said: don't turn on the radio after a
certain time; don't run the bath before or after a certain time; don't
make any noise; the bread is in a certain place or the man across the
way asked who you are. Perhaps she was trying to do a bit of match-
making or maybe she felt like she was reliving a part of her own life.
I found it amusing, and I had kept all those notes until very recently.
They were written in lovely large handwriting, like in the old days. It
was the same school as my mother's because she had exactly the same
way of writing. The capital letters with loops and curlicues, whereas
our writing today is hurried and sloppy. That's how I remember Frau

Savigny. She used to go out when it got cold, and every once in a while she would disappear. I used to ask her why, I had bought a teach-yourself book and liked to try to make myself understood, and she knew a little English. And she told me that she used to go for long walks in the woods. And another time we talked about Spain. I told her that I'd been to Spain, and she asked me if I'd ever been to a bullfight, and I said yes I had and that I'd liked it very much. And then she told me to get out of her house: Since you've been to a bullfight, I no longer want you here. You saw those bulls being killed and I find that horrible. She was raving mad and her eyes had a gleam in them and she kept saying: Get out, get out, I don't want you here. So I told her that it was nice, but that I felt sorry for the poor animals, and I think that calmed her down. She reminded me a little bit of Aigle— Aigle in her later years—and it was difficult for me to get angry with her. I would simply laugh at her idiosyncrasies, but now I think I know what was behind it all. Just as I know in Aigle's case too. I had a dream about her the other day, even though I rarely dream these days. We were crushing grapes, somewhere in Mesogeia, the two of us. We were in a vat, out in the fields, exposed; Aigle had lifted up her skirt round her waist and had nothing on underneath. I want to get a tan, she kept saying: I have to get a tan, look how white my skin is. There she was with her aging sex organ on display, and because I realized there were people watching us, I kept trying to convince her that she couldn't possibly get a tan without any sun. There was just a narrow stream of sunlight filtering through the olive trees, like in summer. But Aigle wouldn't listen. She kept on plunging her feet deeper and deeper into the crushed grapes, like the last dance of a condemned woman, her flabby white thighs trembling, and all she could say in her almost indecent despair was: I have to get a tan, I have to get a tan. One of those dreams that stays with you for days. She was so full of life and she wanted so many things and she would often tell me stories about her love life. She'd say: Hey, Maria, listen, that doctor likes me. He made a pass at me. And she was so old, Aigle,

almost seventy. And she ran around, you know, she was so restless
that nothing could keep her down. Nothing. She had such a lust for
life and she never managed to quell her appetite for it. She was
always on the go, day in and day out, she just never stopped. She
smoked and drank like a maniac and she ate very little, and she would
run around like crazy, painting those nightmarish pictures. She kept
asking me if I liked them. And then one day that roly-poly little
woman decided to take all her paintings and go to America to exhibit
them. She packed them all up and ran around on the subway all by
herself, and she finally did manage to get them hung somewhere and
have her exhibition. She would run up to Kifissia, to her mother, who
was so completely gaga by then that she used to play with her hands,
like they do with little children: Patty-cake, Patty-cake, baker's man,
but in French, of course. That mother of hers, at the age of ninety,
had what they talk about in the Kinsey Report. Which says that after
a certain age women become more senile than men. Mama, she
would ask her pointing at Manos, how old is this man? At that time
Manos was almost forty-five. How old is this gentleman, Mama?
Twenty-seven. And do you like him? She used to use a certain expression, I can't remember it: He's appetizing, she would say. Not appetizing, something else. But it was all so funny with that old lady. Then
I would ask her: Why do they always make you wear that hat? They
always used to make her wear this old-fashioned hat. Because they're
making fun of me, silly girl. She was soft-headed, of course, but every
now and then she had her lucid moments. Because they're making
fun of me, why else do you think they would make me wear that hat?
Then she would lose her train of thought and start in again: Aigle,
how many spoons of sugar do you put in that sweet with the orange
rinds? And she would keep up like that for hours. But what was it that
she used to call Manos? Oh, yes: a real juicy morsel, Aigle, real juicy.
We usually sat on the large balcony and looked out at Pendeli Hill,
the three of us. The four of us. Aigle, her mother, Manos, and I.

She was seventy years old, that Aigle, maybe a little younger, maybe sixty-eight, but she didn't look it. Anyway, she enjoyed my company, maybe because I was Artemis's friend. And then one day she died. Just like that, all alone. By accident. She had hired this English girl, so that there would be someone in the house, because she was so full of anxiety and everything, and then she had this attack and she was in terrible pain. The English girl thought it was her stomach; she must have read somewhere that people with neuroses have stomach trouble, but it was her heart, and she gave her something and she died. She did her in as if she were a rat. Just as well because otherwise it would have been terrible for such an active person to grow old. I cared so much for her, but I didn't go to her funeral. I know it wasn't right, but I wanted to keep her alive, and I refused to go anywhere near her or to ever find out where they had buried her. I wanted to hang on forever to the sound of her voice saying: So, my little Maria, what are we going to do today? That was what she'd say when she'd call me on the phone, and when I remember her it makes me sad. Maybe because now I know what was behind it all. Deep down it was my own panic that kept me away, and it's been quite a few years since she died. Six. But I don't want to say anything else. I'm tired, and when I'm tired my mind starts acting up and I can't speak properly in any language. Because I didn't sleep well last night, because, well, there are just too many becauses, and it's ridiculous, it's comical, when I get blocked like this and have to start using foreign expressions. Of course that can be explained. Your mind just stops working at a certain moment, and if you speak several languages like I do, it's easier to find a word in another language. But you can understand how that makes someone feel. As if you were seeing yourself three times in the same mirror. Like in that poem "Wounded Breakfast." I don't know what's wrong with me, or exactly why my life is the way it is, but look how many things are wrong. The wrong people, the wrong friends, the wrong words, and I realized all

this at the wrong age, too. In other words, too old. I'd rather know
three hundred words and have them be enough for me to get by on.
And not need any other words. Because what is language after all?
A kind of slavery that doesn't set you free, whatever people may say,
and you merely struggle against its tyranny. Like the sea that has been
made into a symbol. It beats against the shores that enclose it, but it
can't get past them, because if it did get past them it would flood
everything and be lost. It beats against them and then gives up,
exhausted, and we think that this is tranquillity when it is really the
deepest kind of despair. Because only within the boundaries defined
by its shores can it exist, but that, too, is just another kind of slavery.
But I have to go now. Nothing is of any interest to me, nothing, since
early this morning. I feel as though I've been emptied of everything,
and I told you that I don't keep accounts with the world, because it
all adds up to nothing in the end, with a remainder of zero. I remember telling you that, and I also feel as if I'm being imprisoned by my
own talkativeness. As though you've set a trap for me. Not that you
forced me to say all these things, because wherever I go all I do is
talk, but you have such a reassuring manner. Especially when you
talked to your mother on the phone. I really liked that, but I don't
believe that's the way you are, I don't believe you're really so calm.
I don't know. Something about you just doesn't fit. I can't say what.
Don't take it the wrong way, because I follow my instincts, and my
instincts have often been wrong. Very wrong, in fact. Anyway, you
have that reassuring manner about you, I wonder why. And what will
you do with all this stuff I'm telling you? I don't think it will be of
much use to you. But I have to go now. Now where did I put that tape
again? I played it back yesterday and my voice sounds lovely. As if I'm
almost pleased with myself for being so unhappy. As if it's the only
thing left that interests me. It's really lovely, my voice, but the way I
keep repeating the words "so much," "so many" and "maybe" and "I
don't know" is tiring, and it bothers me to realize there's so much

uncertainty in me. And then there's the other thing I keep saying about everyone, that "they liked me so much." I don't know. Maybe I should put more order in my thoughts, keep writing them down. But when you read them back they ring false somehow, and then there's that noise of the paper sliding when you turn the page. I'll go to bed now. From my chair to my bed, like it says in that French song: "*De la chaise au fauteuil et du fauteuil au lit*." So many chairs and so many beds from one end of my life to the other. Soon I'll drop off into a faraway slumber. I'll take a pill and I'll fall asleep and I won't wake up, not until the morning. Once the slightest little sound used to send me jumping out of bed. Now I don't hear anything. With pills of course you don't forget, you just fall into a sort of deep, uninterrupted sleep. As if your memory has been temporarily put to one side. But memory can't be put aside. Memory just is.